BLOODWITCH

BOOKS BY AMELIA ATWATER-RHODES

DEN OF SHADOWS

In the Forests of the Night
Demon in My View
Shattered Mirror
Midnight Predator
Persistence of Memory
Token of Darkness
All Just Glass

Poison Tree
Promises to Keep

THE KIESHA'RA

Hawksong
Snakecharm
Falcondance
Wolfcry
Wyvernhail

THE MAEVE'RA TRILOGY

Bloodwitch
Bloodkin
Bloodtraitor

"The Rebel" (a digital original short story)

AMELIA ATWATER-RHODES

BLOODWITCH

THE MAEVE'RA
VOLUME I

EMBER

Text copyright © 2014 by Amelia Atwater-Rhodes
Cover art copyright © 2014 by Sammy Yuen

All rights reserved. Published in the United States by Ember, an imprint of Random House Children's Books, a division of Random House LLC, a Penguin Random House Company, New York. Originally published in the United States by Delacorte Press, an imprint of Random House Children's Books, New York, in 2014.

Ember and the E colophon are registered trademarks of Random House LLC.

randomhouseteens.com

Educators and librarians, for a variety of teaching tools, visit us at RHTeachersLibrarians.com

The Library of Congress has cataloged the hardcover edition of this work as follows:
Atwater-Rhodes, Amelia.
Bloodwitch / Amelia Atwater-Rhodes. — First edition.
pages cm — (Maeve'ra series ; volume 1)
Summary: Raised by vampires, a shapeshifter learns that he may be a bloodwitch who possesses rare and destructive magic that the leader of the powerful Midnight empire seeks to control.
ISBN 978-0-385-74303-7 (hc : alk. paper) — ISBN 978-0-307-98074-8 (ebook)
[1. Fantasy. 2. Shapeshifting—Fiction. 3. Vampires—Fiction. 4. Magic—Fiction.] I. Title.
PZ7.A8925Bl 2014
[Fic]dc23
2013017972

ISBN 978-0-385-74304-4 (trade pbk.)

Printed in the United States of America
10 9 8 7 6 5 4 3 2 1
First Ember Edition 2015

Bloodwitch is dedicated to Tom Hart, 1944-2012.

Fifteen years ago, Tom met a nervous adolescent girl with a book and a dream. Without him, that book would probably have been tucked away in a drawer, unread, unknown, and that dream would have withered away, unlived. You, my reader, would never have turned the pages that took you into Nyeusigrube.

Thank you, Tom. We wouldn't be here without you.

A book starts with an author and an idea, but it doesn't end there. I owe many people for helping me bring *Bloodwitch* from its NaNoWriMo birth to where it is now.

Thank you to Jodi, my editor from the Kiesha'ra series, who came back to work with me on this new project. Her keen eyes and insightful questions always drive me to the edge of despair and panic but also always bring out the best in any book.

More thanks go to Mandi, Bri, Mason, Rayne, Becky, and Ria for multiple read-throughs and invaluable critiques. Some of you put up with only receiving endless variations on the first ten thousand words, for which I am deeply grateful. If it weren't for your comments, I never would have been able to make this world as crisp and defined as it is. Ria, thank you for helping me develop my mad artists, and Mason . . . I owe you. Really. I'm so sorry.

Finally, *Bloodwitch* required more research than anything I have every written, so thank you to everyone who helped me. It's amazing how many commonly used items weren't invented until 1850. A special shout-out goes to Ian Gaudet and all my other Facebook readers for helping me with my horse research. You have all made me want to learn to ride.

Enjoy *Bloodwitch*!

PROLOGUE

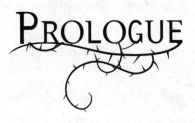

YESTERDAY, AS LADY BRINA worked on her latest masterpiece, she shared with me a myth she had recently learned about quetzals. According to the Mayan people, the bird used to be all green, from the crest on its head to the tip of the male's two-foot-long tail feathers. Almost three hundred years ago, the Mayans fought a great battle against the Spanish. When their greatest warrior, Tecún Umán, was slain, a quetzal settled on his chest to mourn. Tecún's blood stained the bird's breast, leaving the brilliant red feathers that remain today.

The Mayans were not the only ones to recognize the little bird in myths. The Aztecs also revered the resplendent quetzal, with its brilliant red, green, silver, and gold plumes. The male's iridescent green tail feathers were crucial to the Aztecs' sacred rituals, but killing a quetzal was punishable by death, so the great warriors had to capture the birds carefully in order to gently pluck the two long plumes. They then had to release the birds, which could not be kept in captivity.

According to legend, the resplendent quetzal cannot survive in a cage. Romantics say the beautiful bird will die of a broken heart when deprived of its liberty. What is known is that imprisoned quetzals kill themselves.

Lady Brina called the story ironic, though she would not explain why.

Most of the myths she tells are like that. For every moment of love or compassion, there are scenes of brutality and violence. Consider the Greek Prometheus, who was tied to a rock so his liver could be devoured every day for eternity, for the crime of giving fire to humanity. Or poor Hephaestus, who was flung out of Olympus by his own mother for no reason except that he was born ugly.

When Lady Brina paints, she makes these tragic stories beautiful. Even when the subject is dark and terrible, I am drawn to her work. I am grateful to live where I can be surrounded by such beauty all the time.

I do not know why my own parents abandoned me, like the Roman founder Romulus, who was also left in the woods. My guardian, Taro, says that we will probably never know. Maybe I should take a hint from mythology and accept that I was thrown away like Hephaestus. I could have been murdered instead, so my blood would feed the fifth sun, one of the sacrifices the Aztecs believed would keep the world from ending.

My gods, the immortals who have raised and cherished me,

also need blood to survive. I would sacrifice to them if required, but they do not ask it of me. All they ask for is my loyalty and my love.

They have both.

Vance Ehecatl
1803

CHAPTER 1

I DIDN'T MOVE. I didn't dare.

Were my tail feathers trembling? If they weren't already, they would begin to soon. This perch wasn't comfortable, and it was hard to remember why I needed to stay still. It was difficult to understand things like that when I was in my quetzal form.

I risked a quick glance at Lady Brina but saw her brother, Lord Daryl, instead. That was reason enough to freeze. Lady Brina had instructed me to hold this exact pose. Lord Daryl would be very angry if he caught me staring at his sister instead.

I returned my gaze to one of the copper strips that held together the large frosted-glass panels that made up this corner of what Lady Brina called her greenhouse. I had often pondered the name, which seemed strange to me. Lady

Brina's studio was filled with pure white light, and the rest of her "greenhouse" was made of elaborate, multicolored stained-glass mosaics—no more green than any other color. Intricately carved wooden screens let fumes out and fresh air in.

My own two-room wooden cabin was tucked into a corner of the enclosed property, a house inside a house. Sometimes I wondered if the greenhouse was inside *another* house, but I had never been outside it to find out.

My foot slipped again. I had been standing this way for a very long time. I could have slept on one of the perches higher up and been perfectly comfortable, but the steel one Lady Brina had provided near her canvas so I could model for her was slick under my talons. It was hard to find purchase and keep my balance.

I relaxed a little when I realized that Lady Brina was distracted, feeding. I still didn't dare turn my head to look at her, but I could see shadows in my peripheral vision— two women, their forms made giant by the late-afternoon light. I had witnessed similar scenes often enough to know what they meant.

Lady Brina pushed her blood donor away. The second shadow stumbled, and I heard the scuff of a toe against the soft dirt ground. Moments later my shapeshifter friend Calysta crossed my view.

Calysta had promised to give me a dance lesson later, but now she would need to rest instead. I tried to squelch my disappointment. Lady Brina's needs came before my wishes. I would have given her my own blood, if she had asked.

"You need to take a break," Lord Daryl said to his sister.

I needed a break, too, but he wasn't talking to me.

"I just did," Lady Brina replied. I could hear the rattling that meant she was gathering her brushes and tools again.

"I mean you need *rest*," he insisted. "Feeding is important, but so is sleep. You have been in here for two days straight."

"The light is better in the day."

"Two days *and* two nights. I just received the bill for the lamp oil you have burned."

Lady Brina scoffed. I could picture her tossing her hair. It was sleek and black, and reflected every color of light that fell upon her.

"Kendra's yuletide ball is in less than a week," she said, sounding frustrated. If her brother could convince her to take a break, that would be nice. Normally I loved having her near. I loved seeing her, even when she ignored me. But the last day or so, she had been cranky. "She has promised me a place of honor for this piece, and I intend to make sure it is ready. I'm sure you understand."

"Of course I understand."

His voice was soft. I saw their shadows move as he gently removed the brushes and palette from her hands.

"But without sleep, without feeding, without time to rest your eyes on something other than your canvas and oils, how can you possibly *see* your masterpiece anymore? You risk ruining it in your haste to perfect it."

That argument was probably the only one that could have swayed her. She sighed and let Daryl put her tools aside.

Two years ago assistants had helped her erect this canvas, which was twice as high as I was tall, and even wider than that. Occasionally she worked on other, smaller pieces, but inevitably she returned to this massive work. She called it *Tamoanchan*.

I had never been allowed to look at the painting itself, but I had been honored weeks ago when she had asked—no, *ordered*—me to come model. Lady Brina never *asked* anything. That was fine, since I would never have refused her.

Lady Brina had been a frequent presence throughout my life. Even on the days when she failed to acknowledge me at all, which was most days, my beautiful little world seemed to shine brighter when she was around. When she smiled, pleased with the way a particular painting was going, or lay on the soft, dappled grass in the multicolored sunlight, it made my heart beat faster.

At that moment both shadows disappeared. The tingling sensation that always told me when one of their kind was present also faded.

Vampires were able to appear or disappear in the blink

of an eye. The first time it happened near me, I thought I had unexpectedly dozed off and missed Lady Brina's good-bye. I apologized profusely for my rudeness when she returned, and she laughed at me and called me "charming."

Calysta explained that vampires were not like the rest of us. They could do things shapeshifters couldn't. They lived forever, without aging, which was why Brina looked exactly the same now as she had when I was an infant. They were stronger than us, and wiser. That was why they ruled and we were honored to serve.

I fluttered down to the ground, landing awkwardly because of my stupid tail plumes, which had recently started to lengthen and were now twice as long as my bird body. Not wanting to deal with them, I changed into human form quickly . . . though my human form wasn't much better. Growth spurts had left my arms and legs feeling gangly, and even my dance lessons with Calysta couldn't seem to make my limbs work gracefully.

I shook my head, and the leather cord that had been holding my hair back instantly fell out. Though my clothes always reappeared properly when I changed back to human form—trousers, shirt, and sleeveless waistcoat falling tidily into place—I inevitably ended up with a mess of burnt-umber hair in my face.

Every now and then I considered asking Taro to cut it for me, but his hair was long, too. Though his skin was darker than mine, Taro's hair was shiny, coppery-blond, and *always* neat. I needed a comb every time I changed shape. Maybe that was another vampire power, one that Calysta simply hadn't mentioned.

Pushing my hair back uselessly, I took a step toward the painting. I just wanted a peek. Lady Brina had never asked me to model before.

No.

I wasn't supposed to. I wouldn't violate her trust that way. Instead, I did my rounds, occupying my time with responsibilities I had neglected over the last two days as Lady Brina had worked on her painting.

Several small yellow songbirds, an abundance of butterflies, and a hive of honeybees shared the greenhouse with me, along with an assortment of fruit trees, berry bushes, and vines. The orange trees had been ripe for the last month, but I was supposed to gather only one basket of fruit a week, since it would stay fresh on the trees better than it would once harvested.

I searched the ground for any fruit that had fallen, so it wouldn't rot and befoul Lady Brina's greenhouse, and then went to check the stream.

Water welled up on one side from the pores between several large stones, meandered across the greenhouse floor, and then disappeared on the opposite side through another grouping of boulders. The second set of rocks tended to collect debris like leaves, feathers, and misplaced paintbrushes, which I needed to clean out. This time of year the water was frigid when it first bubbled up, but it warmed as it passed over the white stones that lined the streambed. The symbols carved into those stones sparkled as the water flowed over them, creating a warm, golden glow even in the middle of the darkest night.

An animal's shrill cry, carried by the breeze, caused me to lift and then shake my head. Though the glass walls let in plenty of light, even the white ones were so etched and frosted that it was impossible to see through them. The screens allowed gentle breezes to enter the greenhouse but were not conveniently placed for visibility. Sometimes I tried to peer through them, to get a glimpse of the world outside, but they were too high when I was in human form, there were no nearby perches, and my quetzal form did not hover well.

It didn't matter. I had a beautiful world right here. Why did I need anything more?

Taro was adamant that, in addition to my responsibilities taking care of the greenhouse, I needed to take good care of myself. Cleanliness was important, as was exercise. I was supposed to practice my dancing every day, but without Calysta I felt silly when I tried to run through the steps she had taught me. She normally hummed as she danced with me, or played a flute while I danced alone. I would have to wait for her to come back.

I was standing in the doorway of my cabin contemplating what to do next when the door behind me opened with an icy burst of air. Sensing one of *them*, I turned expectantly and smiled to see my guardian, Taro. I started to speak, to greet him and tell him about my day, but then I realized he wasn't alone.

The woman with him reminded me of Lady Brina, but just for a moment, and probably because Lady Brina was the only person I had ever known who seemed so confident in the way she held herself. Like Lady Brina, this woman had fair skin and dark hair, but while Lady Brina's skin was as flawless as the milk-white stones along the streambed, this woman's had a tan hue to it, and while Lady Brina's hair was as black as night, this woman's was a very dark brown. Unlike Lady Brina, who always wore elaborately embroidered gowns, even when she was painting, this woman was wearing a riding habit that stopped above her knees to reveal breeches and tall boots.

My disrespectful eyes snapped to the ground as soon as I realized I was staring. The woman before me was obviously a vampire. I could feel the way her power resonated in my head and along my skin. I didn't need to look at her eyes to see if they were black, like those of all her kind. I *shouldn't*; it wasn't my place to meet her gaze. Instead, I did what Taro had taught me to do whenever I met one of them: I lowered my knees to the ground, bowed my head, and waited to be acknowledged.

"Mistress Jeshickah," Taro said to the woman, "may I present Vance Ehecatl."

Mistress Jeshickah! My heart leapt into my throat, and I fought the desire to raise my head and get a better look at her. Taro referred to her frequently as my benefactor and the most powerful woman in the world, but I had never met her. Mistress Jeshickah was the only woman whom even Lady Brina spoke of with awe.

I didn't have to wait long. She reached out and placed a finger under my chin, drawing me to my feet and raising my head with the pressure of one sharp nail.

Don't speak unless spoken to, I reminded myself. But I had so many things I wanted to say! So many questions!

"You're certain he is fourteen?" she asked Taro as she examined my face.

"Yes," Taro replied. "I know he appears young for his age, but I have been told that is common with the breed."

"True. Jaguar's Celeste is almost sixteen now but could pass for twelve," she remarked. Was she talking about another, female quetzal? If so, where was she? She didn't live in my home. Were there two places like this?

"They all mature, with time," he said.

I stumbled when Mistress Jeshickah released me. She turned back to Taro. "I had to speak to Brina," she said. "She was talking about her model at the market, of all places. Do you still feel this is the best place for him?"

Alarm shot through me. Where else would I go?

"He's happy here," Taro said, placing a comforting hand on my shoulder. "And even the merchants are used to Brina's stories. No one pays her much mind. They won't believe she actually has a quetzal here."

"I've doubled the guards on the door, all the same."

I bit my tongue to hold back yet more questions. Lady Brina had been talking about me! Why was that a bad thing? A *dangerous* thing, perhaps, which necessitated additional guards.

"I think it might be worth finding someone who can—" Taro paused, glancing at me. "We should probably continue this conversation later," he said. "Vance is easily overwhelmed by big ideas. There's no need to trouble him. Right, Vance?"

He looked at me as he said that, but I wasn't sure how to respond, so I just said, "Right."

"Keep me updated," Mistress Jeshickah said to Taro.

Then she disappeared without another word.

"She didn't even say hello," I said plaintively.

Taro's gaze snapped to mine, the disappointment on his face sharp enough to cut as he barked, *"Vance!"*

Shame crept over me. I ducked my head, whispering, "I'm sorry." I knew I shouldn't criticize any of them, *especially* her. Mistress Jeshickah ran Midnight, the empire that provided for all my needs. She was a busy woman. I added, "I just wanted to say thank you." My real mother had abandoned me as a baby. I would have died if Mistress Jeshickah hadn't taken me in.

Taro patted my shoulder sympathetically. "You say

thank you by showing you were raised right and acting with proper respect. She doesn't need your words." As I pondered that kernel of wisdom, he added, "You did well, Vance."

The praise made me smile, but the expression faded as I considered what I had heard. "Is Lady Brina in danger?" I asked.

"No," Taro answered. After a pause he said, "Not much, anyway, but she could be if the wrong people learned of your presence here. Until you are older and more able to protect yourself—and your lady—it would be best if you kept your head down."

"Who would want to hurt us?"

"The world out there," he said, waving in the general direction of the doorway, "is a dangerous place, Vance. Mistress Jeshickah does her best to keep the more violent elements under control, but there are always some who insist on striking out against those of us who try to keep order. They know they cannot harm one of our kind, but some of them might be tempted to hurt someone they see as dear to us. Do you understand?"

I nodded gravely. I had never considered the lengths to which my guardians went to keep me safe, and secret. I resolved to repay them all somehow, someday.

CHAPTER 2

THE DAY, WHICH had begun so beautifully, turned stormy as evening approached. Sleet cascaded against the roof and walls like hammer blows. Though magic kept the greenhouse warm, the noise outside was enough to keep me awake deep into the night.

I was curled up in bed, trying to sleep, when I heard one of the birds call a staccato greeting. Someone was here.

I stood, crossed the kitchen, and opened the front door of my cabin, peering through the darkness.

"Be *careful* with that!"

Brina's cross voice was music to my ears. I wasn't eager for another two-day modeling session, but even that was better than doing nothing but lying in bed and listening to the pounding weather. I dressed quickly and hurried to greet her.

She hadn't made it much past the doorway by the time I arrived. I was startled to see a man I didn't recognize, in addition to the usual bevy of slaves carrying her materials and Calysta carrying the more valuable tools.

This wasn't the first time Lady Brina had brought a stranger into the greenhouse, but it was a rare occurrence, and I found it unnerving, coming so close on the heels of my ominous conversation with Taro.

He didn't look like anyone I had ever seen. His hair, which was braided into a long tail, was white as ice. When he glanced up at me, I saw that his eyes were a pale blue-green. He obviously wasn't a vampire, but I doubted he was human. A shapeshifter, like me? Or he could be a witch; I had never seen one of those, but I had heard about them, both in myth and in Lord Daryl's complaints about the fees they charged for working in the greenhouse.

All the stranger's clothing was well fitted, every piece fastened neatly. Except for the brown boots that rose to his knees and a few errant straps and buckles, his entire out-fit was made of white or off-white fur and leather, giving him the appearance of something crafted out of the same frosted, colorless glass that surrounded Lady Brina's studio.

The man had placed his heavy-looking bag on the ground and opened the top as if searching for something.

"I have a good quantity of *azul Maya*," he said, "which, as you know, is far preferable to Alexandria blue. I also have a quantity of silver cochineal."

"These are Azteka pigments!" Lady Brina exclaimed. "How do you have them?"

"I'm resourceful," he replied. "It is five days until Kendra's famous art exhibition. Should I assume you want them?"

"Yes, yes," Lady Brina said, her gaze already turned impatiently toward her studio area.

"Would the lovely, talented lady mind if I stayed here for a few hours, until the storm passes?" the merchant pressed. "If this weather spoils my other wares, I might not be able to—"

"*Fine,*" Lady Brina snapped. "I need to get to work. Calysta, write the man a receipt to present to my secretary for payment. Vance, help me with this lamp oil."

I sprang forward, happy to assist and to get a better look at the stranger. Upon closer inspection it was obvious that every inch of him was soaked to the bone. There were small crystals of ice still melting in the folds of the heavy cloak he had discarded before looking through his pack. No wonder he wanted to get out of the storm.

He paid almost no attention to me. When his gaze drifted idly past mine, I ducked my head to hide my face and picked up one of the heavy crates of lamp oil—enough to burn for a century, it seemed. Calysta stepped forward and drew back the hood of her cloak, shaking water away.

I was turning to leave when I heard the stranger say in a horrified, strangled tone, "*You're* Calysta?"

"Sir?" she replied.

The stranger was staring, every muscle tensed, his eyes wide. A moment later Lady Brina glanced back with a huff, obviously frustrated that I had stopped.

"Is there a problem, Obsidian?" Lady Brina asked coolly. "You're distracting my boy."

The stranger—Obsidian, she'd called him—shook himself and turned to look away from Calysta. "This woman . . . ?"

"She's on loan from Taro," Lady Brina answered. "She is teaching my boy to dance, since that's something her kind has a talent for. She also has a tolerable knowledge of art."

"I know," Obsidian whispered.

"Come, Vance," Lady Brina said, drawing me toward her. She set a hand on my back as I caught up, and said, "We have work to do."

We worked together to fill and light the many lamps Lady Brina required when she worked at night and in weather such as this. As I carefully funneled oil into the elaborate glass contraptions, each handmade by Lord Daryl, Lady Brina mixed pigments and considered her canvas.

"*Tamoanchan* is what the human Aztecs—the Mexica, as they name themselves—call their afterlife," she mused. "It is a paradise, full of fountains, rivers, and forests. At its center is the flowering tree of life, where all life began, which means this painting needs to tell not only the story of what happens after death but also what happened at the *beginning*. I suppose it's your myth, as well, since your kind comes from the same origins."

"What origins?" I asked cautiously. Sometimes if I interrupted her, she would stop talking, especially if she had a brush in her hand. But when she was preparing her studio, she usually enjoyed questions.

"According to the Mexica," she explained, "when the god Huitzilopochtli guided his people from their mythical homeland, his sister, Malinalxochitl, traveled with them. She was a great sorcereress, who could take the form of a bird or an animal, cause madness with a look, or shake a river from its course through her will alone. The priests feared her power and begged Huitzilopochtli to control her. In response the great god of war and death drugged his sister and left her behind when the rest of the Mexica moved on." She cast a sideways glance my way, along with a soft smile. "Men fear women with power, you see."

I contemplated that notion as Lady Brina adjusted the lamps. Taro was always courteous to Lady Brina, and of course his respect for Mistress Jeshickah bordered on awe, but did he *fear* them? Was I supposed to?

Lady Brina did not elaborate. Instead, she fiddled with the mirrors that reflected and increased the light, and then continued her story. "Those loyal to Malinalxochitl stayed with her. The Mexica were mostly destroyed when the Spanish came to their shores, but Malinalxochitl's people had their sorcery to protect them. They became the Azteka, and they are still a powerful nation, populated by jaguar and quetzal shapeshifters. They're almost as powerful as Midnight, or so *they* seem to think." Another of those conspiratorial smiles. "If they are so powerful, though, I don't see why they would have abandoned a baby in the woods."

"Why do you think they did?" I asked, but Lady Brina had already picked up her brush. An expression of fierce concentration settled on her face as she slipped into her own personal world. She would be lost to everything but her painting for a while now, including Calysta, who came to report that Obsidian was asleep and under guard.

"Is he dangerous?" I asked her in the hushed tone we both instinctively fell into when Lady Brina was working.

"He could be if he wanted to," Calysta answered, "but even Malachi Obsidian knows better than to cross—" She broke off and frowned, as if a thought had come to her briefly and then been lost. "He wouldn't hurt you, but you should still stay away. He's a liar, and no good for anyone."

"He acted as if he knew you," I remarked. *And you know more of his name than Lady Brina used.*

"Maybe, long ago," Calysta answered with a shake of her head. "Not now."

"Is he a serpent, like you? Are you from the same place?" Lady Brina's tale had made me curious. Normally the myths she told me were about places like Greece and Rome, places that had no connection to my world.

Almost as powerful as Midnight, or so they *seem to think.*

Midnight was the pinnacle of civilization. How could the Azteka think they were anywhere near as good? Did others think the same about themselves?

"Yes—no," Calysta answered. "It's complicated, and it doesn't matter. I come from a place where it is often cold, and wet, and an empty stomach is more common than a full one. Why do you think Malachi wanted to get inside? Why do you think your mother left you for Midnight to have? This is a better life." She gave a full-body shiver, as if trying to shake off the last of the chill from outside. With what looked like a forced smile, she said, "Dance with me, Vance."

"What did Lady Brina mean when she said you were on loan from Taro?"

Human slaves, like the cook and the maid, could be borrowed or loaned, but Calysta was a shapeshifter, like me. She wasn't a slave, was she? Could shapeshifters *be* slaves?

"Taro asked me to come here," Calysta answered. "About two years ago now. Do you remember? You told him you felt lonely when Lady Brina wasn't around. He thought you should have a companion." She smiled and caught my hands. "This is a beautiful place, Vance. Don't sully it by dwelling on the dark things. Please," she added, her voice soft and imploring.

A place where it is often cold, and wet, and an empty stomach is more common than a full one. I felt bad, forcing her to dwell on such terrible memories, so I dropped the conversation and let her guide me. I had been learning some new steps, which my body didn't quite believe were possible yet.

The sun had come up, and I had almost mastered the tricky move, by the time Lady Brina announced, "Done. It's done. Finally. Come see, Vance," she said. "I think it's my best work yet."

As I reached Lady Brina, she set a hand on my hair, ruffling it and inevitably getting multicolored paint in the dark strands. The glowing, exhausted, yet triumphant smile on her face was more than sufficient reward for the last several days' crankiness.

The central image in the painting was a giant tree, which had been cleft down the middle. Blood flowed from the center, but each side continued to grow, the trunks spiraling around each other. The tree was full of jewels, blooming with dozens of different types of flowers, and brilliant green feathers fell around it like rain. In the sky above a quetzal spread its wings and soared.

Me, I thought.

My chest grew tight, and tears filled my eyes. The tiny bird, with its red breast and long, green tail feathers, seemed so free. Triumphant. Powerful, and joyous, and—

Next to me, Calysta let out a strangled sound. She asked, "Lady Brina, do you want me to clean up for you, so you can rest?"

I stared at Calysta, startled by the interruption. I could

24

have continued staring at the painting for hours, but despite the small sound that had escaped her just moments ago, Calysta's downcast eyes showed no emotion.

"Yes, that would be good," Lady Brina said. "I feel like I could sleep for a century, but I suppose I shall settle for closing my eyes until sundown."

She disappeared without another word.

"I will take care of the mess," Calysta said to me as soon as Lady Brina was gone. "You should get some rest, too. You haven't slept any more than Lady Brina."

I nodded. "Are you sure you don't need help?"

"I'm fine." She turned her back on me, so I walked away.

I needed to sleep—now that I paused to think about it, I could feel how heavy my body was—but I also felt restless. I wanted to go look at the painting again, but I didn't want to get in Calysta's way.

I took my quetzal form and flew up to the highest perch, instead, where I sat next to a small songbird for a while. It hopped off the perch, circled, landed, circled again, landed again. I watched it, wondering what it would say if it could talk to me. Unfortunately, even in bird form my mind was too human to communicate with my always-feathered companions.

I returned to the ground and paced in a circle. Why did my greenhouse suddenly feel so *small*? Why could I not get the image of that painted quetzal, flying above a flowering tree full of jewels and blood, out of my head?

I walked to the stream and knelt to dip my hands in the cool water.

Without quite knowing why, I found my hands closing around one of the rocks on the streambed. Impulse took me, and with a quetzal's short, quavering cry, I flung the stone with all my strength.

The instant it was out of my hand, I realized my heart was pounding in my throat. How would I explain the shattered glass? Worse, how would I explain why I had damaged the beautiful stained-glass mosaic?

I flinched in anticipation of a crash that never came.

The stone bounced off the magic-imbued glass, which sparkled in the aftermath of the blow.

I looked around guiltily, but no one had seen. The stranger was still sleeping near the doorway, Calysta was still cleaning the studio, and no one else was around.

What was I *doing*?

And *why*?

I felt so lost.

CHAPTER 3

I CRAWLED INTO my bed and dragged an extra blanket over myself, afraid to do anything else. I tried to breathe slowly, to calm my racing heart, but I ended up tossing and turning all night. When I woke the storm had let up, though the light that made its way through the greenhouse walls still had a cool, gray quality to it.

I went to the stream, where I stripped and submerged myself in the warm waters. The restless night had left all my muscles tense. I didn't see anyone on my way there or back—Malachi, or Calysta—and for the moment I was glad to be alone.

I retreated to my house, dried off, and dressed again. I waved the cook away and set to baking bread, hoping the usually soothing, rhythmic work of kneading the dough would help calm me, but the stickiness and the bittersweet smell of the sourdough culture only made my stomach turn and the crawling sensation along my arms dig its way deeper into my muscles.

I left the bread to rise and examined the guarded door to the world beyond my greenhouse, wondering what would happen if I tried to leave. The guards were protecting the greenhouse from something outside, right? Not guarding *me*. Maybe I could just walk up and open the door. Peek outside. I didn't want to leave. I just wanted to look. That couldn't be too dangerous, could it?

I hoped Taro would come that evening so I could talk to him more about the outside world and what my role in it was. He had talked about my learning to protect myself and Lady Brina. Did that mean he would teach me to fight? To be a guard?

When sunset passed with no sign of Taro, I approached the greenhouse door again. It would have been unusual for him to come two nights in a row, but I had so been hoping. . . .

I knew the guards were standing just outside, but I couldn't see them through the colored glass. I might as well have been alone in the world. Would the door open if I pushed it? All at once, I was sure it wouldn't. I was locked in. Trapped.

Lady Brina's amused voice fluttered through my mind: *They say a quetzal can't survive in a cage. Ironic, isn't it?*

Heart pounding so hard I was dizzy from it, I reached for the door, lifted the latch, and shoved.

Frigid air whipped around me. The world outside my greenhouse was apparently dark and freezing. I wrapped my arms around my chest and hunched my head down against the wet-and-cold that was falling from the sky.

Snow, I told myself. Calysta had described it to me once. It had sounded pretty then. Now it was just cold. I started shivering immediately and had to keep blinking water out of my eyelashes. How could people survive out here?

The four guards all tensed, spinning toward me. One asked, "Is everything all right, sir?"

I swallowed the lump in my throat and asked, "Am I allowed to leave?"

They exchanged meaningful glances. One said, "We've been ordered to protect this door, sir, not to keep anyone from leaving."

The darkness seemed to press in around me. One of the guards held a lamp, but it did little to illuminate more than a hint of the path near us.

"Which way would I go?" I asked.

"The path divides," one of the guards answered. "To the north it goes toward the di'Birgetta estate. To the west it goes toward the market, and Midnight proper."

The di'Birgetta estate had to be where Lady Brina and Lord Daryl lived. I didn't know what the other two places were.

One of the guards added, "You wouldn't want to go as you are now, sir. You would freeze to death."

He was right. The guards were all wearing heavy clothes: cloaks, boots, gloves, and hats. I was shivering against the wind, even though I could still feel the magically warm air of the greenhouse at my back.

"Is it always like this out here?" I asked. I had thought the storm was over, but there was still snow falling.

"Not always," the guards answered, "but it *is* winter."

I was just about to turn around and go back inside, thanking the fates that I didn't need to go out in that disgusting weather, when I saw lights approaching from the direction the guard had called north. As they drew closer, I saw Lady Brina's studio slaves.

"Is Lady Brina coming back tonight?" I asked the guards.

"Yes, she is," one answered me. "We've been ordered to tidy the studio and start the lamps so she can reveal her completed masterpiece to Lord Daryl."

He had barely finished speaking when Lady Brina herself appeared in the doorway, inches away from me. I jumped back. Since she appeared under the awning and hadn't needed to hike through the woods, she was perfectly dry—a sharp contrast to my own damp and shivering state.

"Boy, you're a mess," she chastised me. "Soaking wet. Go pretty yourself up before you embarrass me."

The words brought a bright flush to my face, and I hurried back to my cabin to dry off and put on fresh clothes. I was pulling on a shirt when Lady Brina screamed. The noise made the glass around us ring in response and shocked the last of the chill from my blood. I raced toward her, vaulting the stream when I came to it and ignoring the branches that whipped my face when I failed to duck in time.

The smell hit me first as I reached the alcove where Brina did her work. The noxious odor coming from the dimly lit clearing assaulted my nose and made me stagger backward. I couldn't identify it; it was like nothing I had ever smelled before. I had to force myself forward, but every instinct made me want to recoil and vomit.

Brina was holding a lamp up in front of her canvas, trembling.

"It's . . . it's . . ."

"My lady, what's wrong?" I asked. I couldn't see the canvas itself, and I was afraid to walk around to get a better look.

"Ruined," she said. "It's ruined."

A fly rose up and settled on her cheek, making her shriek again and fall back. I caught her arm, trying to stabilize her, but she shoved me away, sending me sprawling backward, too. I landed hard on my left hand, twisting my wrist, and yelped in pain.

"How *dare* she?" Brina whispered, spinning away. She walked toward her easel again, running her fingers through her black hair, pulling out the combs and sticks that had held it up.

I stood cradling my hurt hand, then approached. I tried not to smell . . . whatever it was.

My first thought was that Calysta had spilled paint all over many of Lady Brina's brushes and splashed it on her masterpiece. No wonder she was furious.

I moved closer, wondering if I could clean anything up. If the paint was still wet, I might be able to . . .

To . . .

Might be able . . .

My mind took it all in very slowly, protective instincts trying to shield me as the rest of my brain attempted to make sense of what I was seeing.

Calysta was lying, very still and very pale, on the ground.

In one of her hands was one of Lady Brina's palette knives, made sharp by many years of use on rough pigments.

In her opposite wrist was another palette knife. In her *wrist*. Stuck there.

And all around her was blood. Not paint. Blood.

I staggered backward as the word came to me: *dead*.

Calysta was dead. Probably had been since I had left her alone that morning. She stank. There were flies on her.

She had done it herself. There was no other explanation.

Why?

I staggered away and sought Lady Brina. She was a worldly woman. She had to have some kind of explanation.

"Why would she kill herself?" I asked. Lady Brina was looking at me with wide, shocked eyes. My impulse was to hold and comfort her, but at the same time *I* wanted to be comforted. "How could I not have known? Why—"

I reached for Brina, and she responded so fast I had no idea her hand was coming until it struck me. I fell to the ground again, my jaw throbbing as I stared up at her in confusion.

"How *dare* you try to claim sympathy for yourself? Do you have any idea how valuable those brushes were? Or—" She wailed, "My painting. My beautiful *Tamoanchan*."

"My lady," I said softly, "I'm sorry that I—"

She cut off my apologetic words with a sharp kick to my ribs. "You *should* be sorry!" she shouted. "I didn't want you here in the first place, cluttering my greenhouse, but one doesn't refuse a request from Mistress Jeshickah. Now you've brought this *mess*. Fix it."

She stormed out, leaving me curled on the ground, trying to breathe past the agony in my chest. What had I done?

It took me three tries to get to my feet, and then I didn't know what to do with myself. I was confused, hurt, and in pain, and I didn't know what to do about any of that. I felt tears filling my eyes, and I blinked rapidly to keep them dry. Crying was unacceptable. Taro had taught me that long ago.

I stared at the painting. Brina had said to fix it, but

how? It wasn't just the blood. Calysta had sliced all the way through the canvas itself, savagely destroying the beautiful work.

Calysta was staring at me, her wide, sapphire-blue eyes filmed over by death. I tried to shut them, but they flew back open. I couldn't even get the knife out of her wrist. She had driven it in too deep, and pulling at it made my stomach roll. I fetched a blanket from my cabin and wrapped her in it, then turned to the painting, wondering if there was anything I could do. I dabbed at the congealed blood with a cloth.

I saw nothing, heard nothing, before strong hands picked me up and flung me backward with a force so powerful my body and head hit the wall. I saw stars as I fell. The magic made the glass shimmer and wail as it absorbed the impact—better than my body did.

I looked up to find Lord Daryl standing above me, fuming. He demanded, "What did you do to Brina?"

"I didn't do anything," I protested.

His knee striking my jaw bowled me over. My teeth cut the inside of my cheek, filling my mouth with the coppery taste of blood.

"I didn't do anything," I said again. It hurt to talk, but I needed to convince him. "I'm sorry. I would never want to make her unhappy. Calysta killed herself. I don't know why. She tore up the painting. I didn't do anything."

Except upset her by asking about Malachi, and her past. If I had been left alone with the painting, what would I have done? More than throw a rock.

My tormentor turned when I mentioned the painting, seeing it in full for the first time. The instant his attention was off me, I changed into quetzal shape. Panicked, I darted past him.

I heard him curse, and he reached for me, but all he caught was one tail feather, which ripped off in his hand. I struggled for a moment, off balance, but managed to get enough air under my wings to lift me higher than he could reach.

I fled to a perch as close to the ceiling of my world as I could get, though it made me achingly aware of the wood and glass panels that limited my upward flight.

Below, I saw Lord Daryl looking up at me, furious. Eventually he dropped the feather and went back to the painting, calling slaves toward him as he went and giving them instructions.

He raised his gaze to me one more time and said clearly, "We will finish this conversation," before he disappeared.

I had absolutely no desire *ever* to finish this particular conversation.

The stench of Calysta's corpse still enveloped me, and the taste of blood lingered in my mouth. My tiny bird's body still hurt.

I dropped to the ground and changed into human form. It hurt to walk, and I was shaking so badly I was afraid I would fall down, but I forced myself to keep moving. The two guards normally positioned by the door were lying very still, their eyes open and staring. They must have tried to stop Lord Daryl from entering in a rage.

That meant they had died protecting me.

Whispering an apology and a plea for forgiveness, I tugged a cloak away from one of the guards and wrapped it around my own shoulders. I couldn't stand to try to pull the gloves off his dead fingers, though I knew I would probably regret my squeamishness. I did take the still-burning whale-oil lantern.

I had to talk to Taro and could only hope that the west path the guards had mentioned would take me to him, or someone who could get word to him.

Lady Brina doesn't want me here. The knowledge brought a lump to my throat. I couldn't imagine leaving the beautiful greenhouse in favor of the outside world, where it was cold and miserable, but I couldn't stay if she didn't want me to.

Maybe later I could find her and explain, and ask forgiveness. She had been upset and had lashed out. . . .

No. She wouldn't have hurt me that way if she cared about me the way I cared about her. I was a nuisance. *Clutter.* Only there because Mistress Jeshickah wanted me there.

Once again I choked back the lump in my throat. It was too cold to cry anyway.

CHAPTER 4

THE INSTANT I stepped beyond the sphere of the greenhouse's magic, the wind sucked the breath from my lungs and replaced it with ice.

I slogged ahead, lifting my lantern to try to illuminate the fork in the path in front of me. I turned resolutely in the direction I hoped would take me to Taro, only to start second-guessing myself within moments. I had no idea how far away the market or Midnight proper, the two places the guards had mentioned, could be.

It was so *dark*.

I hadn't gone far before the darkness overwhelmed the light. The trees above were ominous, reaching creatures, blocking the moonlight.

Maybe I could see more if I took to the air. I could probably also travel faster by wing. I could be there before

I knew it. I set the lantern down, changed shape, and beat my wings frantically as I sought the open sky.

Icy wind whipped me around, buffeting my unpracticed wings around like leaves. I tumbled through the air, struggling to regain control, and eventually landed back on the ground with a thud. A bank of snow broke my fall, but that was the only comfort I had. I changed back into human form, miserably aware that I was no longer on the path. I didn't even know where my lantern was.

I hugged my cloak more tightly around myself and limped onward, feeling every bruise keenly.

As soon as Taro realized I was missing, he would come looking for me. Right? In the meantime, though, I couldn't stop moving. It was too cold.

I grabbed a fallen stick and used it to drag a trail in the dirt and snow around me as I walked. Occasionally I made arrow marks to indicate my direction. I thought about adding my name—Calysta had shown me how to write it once—but couldn't remember all the marks required. Instead, I took my quetzal form just long enough to reach back with my beak and pluck a tail feather. After I returned to human form, I stuck the long feather in the snow so that it poked up where it seemed most visible.

There. If anyone saw it, they would follow the trail to find me.

Feeling better about my chances, if not any warmer, I started out.

At first I sang as I walked, but then singing reminded me of Calysta, which made my throat tight and made me feel even colder, so I stopped. When I was silent, though, every noise around me made me jump. Distant crashing sounded like a monster. And was that a roar? What lived in this forest?

That roar could have belonged to a lion or a jaguar. My neck ached from trying to look all ways at once, including up, since jaguars could attack from the trees. What about wolves or bears?

Lady Brina loved to talk about savage beasts, which she found beautiful and exotic. I had never asked *where* they existed, because all that mattered to me was that they didn't exist in *my* world.

I yelped as a figure emerged from the forest's shadows, like a ghost stepping into my path. I raised my stick, then set it back down as I realized he was a man, not a monster, holding a small lamp that illuminated little beyond our feet.

"I thought I heard someone stumbling around." He raised the lamp. "Aren't you Brina's boy?"

The light was in my eyes, but I finally recognized Malachi Obsidian, the trader who had come by the greenhouse the day before.

"My name is Vance," I said. "You're Malachi, right?"

"This isn't the safest area to wander, Vance," he replied.

"If it's not safe, what are you doing here?" I asked defensively, one breath before I realized his words could have been a threat instead of a warning. Though his hands were empty at the moment, he had a slender sword—really more of a long dagger—at his left hip, and a bow and quiver on his back.

The retort apparently took him aback. He frowned and said, "You're not broken."

"Not *what*?" I hoped he could help me find my way home, but the intensity of his stare was making me uncomfortable.

"Are you a slave?" he asked.

"No!" I said vehemently, before I remembered what Lady Brina had said about Calysta: *on loan from Taro*. Had she been a slave? "And I'm allowed to be out here. I'm just lost."

"Are you happy?" he asked. Seeing my look, he added, "Not right now, obviously. I mean when you're at the greenhouse. Are you happy there?"

"Yes," I answered, grateful for an easier question. I almost added more, about the things that had just happened—the painting, Calysta, Lady Brina, and Lord Daryl's rage—but I bit my lip. I had lived there for fourteen years, and nothing like this had ever happened before.

"Then I'll help you find your way back. In the morning," he added firmly. "It's pitch-black out here. You can come to my camp for the night. I have enough dinner to share."

My stomach chose that moment to growl, reminding

me that it had been a long time since I had eaten more than a few bites of bread. It had been easy to ignore while I wandered lost and frightened, but I wasn't going to turn down food.

"Thank you," I said, trying to recall all of Taro's lessons on proper manners. "I appreciate the help."

He snickered at my attempt to be polite and turned to lead the way. One step later he paused to look back and say, "No, leave the stick. We don't want to encourage anyone else to find us."

I gripped my stick more tightly despite my cold fingers. "But I *want* to be found!" I argued.

"In this forest all sorts of things could come looking for you. I'm not going to force you to follow me," he said, "but I'm not going to let you leave a path to my camp, either. Make up your mind."

He turned and started to walk away without giving me a chance to decide. What if Malachi Obsidian was one of those people Taro had talked about who could be a danger to me? I had no way of knowing. What I did know for certain was that starving and freezing were bad, which meant I didn't have a choice. I dropped the stick and followed my new guide through the trees.

Rustling nearby caused him to halt, his hand moving slowly toward his bow.

I came up beside him and saw what had made the noise: a sleek-coated stag, standing like a statue, staring at our light with its black-tipped tail raised in alarm. He could have stepped directly out of Lady Brina's painting of Artemis, the goddess of the hunt. She had worked on that series, which she called Proud Ladies, as long as she had worked on *Tamoanchan*.

My guts twisted at the reminder. The painting. Calysta. The guards.

A small sound escaped my throat, and the stag bolted.

"We couldn't hunt it anyway," my guide said with a sigh. He continued walking, speaking without looking at me. "Jeshickah has some very old-world laws regarding deer on her land."

I stumbled, so shocked by his words that I lost my footing and fell, letting out a yelp as my bare hands landed in the snow.

Malachi paused and grasped my arm to help me up. "You all right?" he asked.

Never, *never* in my life had I heard Mistress Jeshickah referred to without a title. If I had done so, or even spoken of Lady Brina that way, Taro would have slapped me. I would have deserved it. How *dare* he?

I opened my mouth to challenge him—and then shut it fast, dropping my gaze. I was at his mercy for the moment. "I'm fine," I answered. "I tripped on . . . on a rock."

He hadn't apologized for the slip or questioned my lie about why I fell, which meant . . . he didn't expect me to care. My mind turned that thought over like a pebble, because it wasn't quite right.

Malachi knew where I came from. He had thought I was a slave, but now he knew that I was happy with Lady Brina. He should expect me to care.

Was he testing me?

"We're here," Malachi announced, interrupting my train of thought.

"Where?" I asked. I saw nothing but more trees and brush, covered in the seemingly endless snow.

"*Here,*" he said, putting an arm across my shoulders to usher me forward.

The camp, invisible just a moment before, was suddenly clear as daylight. A grove of birch trees ringed the small clearing, at the center of which a covered cooking pot sat on merrily glowing coals. Most of the snow within the grove had been packed down or brushed away, leaving a smooth-topped log near the fire for a seat. The tent emerged from the space beyond like something organic, half buried in the snow, with a small gap open to the warmth of the fire.

Magic, I thought. Was Malachi a witch? All I knew about them I had learned from overheard complaints from Lord Daryl and Lady Brina. Witches were greedy, mercenary creatures. They were needed for things like the spells on the greenhouse, but they couldn't be trusted.

"Did Brina send you away, or did you go on your own?" Malachi asked casually as he lifted the copper lid to check on his food.

Lady Brina, I thought instinctively. A few minutes ago the guilty fear in my gut would have forced the whole story out like a confession. Now I didn't trust this man enough to want to share the horrors of the last few hours.

I settled for a half truth. "I tried to go for a walk," I answered. "I got lost."

My host looked up, sea-foam eyes piercing. I braced myself, expecting to be accused of lying. Instead, he asked, "How old are you?"

Mistress Jeshickah had said I looked younger than I was. A younger child would be more likely to get lost, right? Being younger could give me an excuse for a lot of silly slipups I might make. "Eleven," I answered.

"Hmm." He turned back to the fire. "Were you on your way to the market?"

"I don't—I mean, yes, I was." That was the way I was heading, anyway, though it wasn't my actual goal. I didn't want to tell him I'd been looking for Taro.

Again, those eyes on me, intense . . . and then sparkling, as he chuckled and shook his head.

"Truce," he said, amusement still in his voice. "I'll share my squirrel stew and stop asking questions if you stop pretending you know how to lie."

"I—I don't know what—" I stammered. "I mean—" He quirked a brow, waiting for me to get my tongue untangled. Finally, I gave up on defending myself and asked, "What's a squirrel?"

"It's—" This time he was the one who seemed speechless. I had meant to ask something benign, not something that was apparently shocking. "A small animal with a bushy tail," he said at last. "The next time I see one, I'll point it out." Were squirrels common out here? Lady Brina cared more about gods and goddesses than bushy-tailed little animals, and she had never mentioned them. "Take a seat," he urged, gesturing toward the tree trunk. "Dinner's ready. I even have an extra bowl in my pack."

The pack in question was hanging from one of the tree branches. I didn't know if it had been as invisible as the campsite was earlier, or if I just hadn't been paying attention.

My host handed me a tin bowl of stew and a clunky spoon, then filled a second bowl, folded his legs under himself, and sat on the snow near the fire. Since the snow wasn't falling anymore, I pushed my hood back to get it out of the way as I ate what turned out to be a surprisingly tasty meal. Whatever "squirrel" was, it made good stew.

When I asked for seconds, however, my host said, "Only if I get to ask another question."

I could always refuse to answer, if I needed to. "Okay."

"Are you a bloodwitch?"

I recognized the word "witch," but I didn't know the rest of the term he used. "Am I a what?"

"You're a quetzal, right?" he asked. When I hesitated, he said, "I could tell you were a bird the first time I saw you, but I wasn't paying much attention, so I figured a crow or a raven. The feathers give you away." He gestured to the back of his neck, causing me to reach instinctively toward mine. I didn't think about the feathers that grew at the nape of my neck often, because they didn't get in my face like my hair did. I knew they were red and green like gemstones, though. Apparently they were visible by firelight.

Since there was obviously no hiding it, and I didn't know why I would need to, I admitted, "Yes, I'm a quetzal. But if one of us is a witch, I think it's you." I remembered the way the entire camp had seemed to materialize only when he put his hand on my shoulder.

"Why does Brina have a quetzal?" he asked.

I didn't want to answer any more questions, and he had already said he wouldn't ask. "I don't need thirds," I answered dryly, which made him laugh again.

"Fine, fine," he said. "I'll help you home tomorrow, and accept that some secrets are in my best interests."

He had accused me of being a bad liar, but I suspected Malachi Obsidian was probably a very good liar. Calysta had said as much. His attitude had changed when he realized I was a quetzal. I wasn't sure I trusted his offer to get me home anymore.

No, my best course now was to wait for him to sleep, then set out again, leaving behind this stranger with his unsettling gaze and prying questions. Maybe he was harmless, but my gut said otherwise.

Taro and the others would be looking for me by now; I was sure of it. But, they might not be able to find me in Malachi's magically hidden campsite, which was why I needed to get away.

"Can we sleep?" I asked, pushing away the half-full bowl of stew. His questioning had ruined what appetite I had left, and I wanted an excuse for the conversation to be over. "I was in the woods a long time."

"Of course," he answered. "The tent will be close quarters with two of us, but that keeps it warmer. I'm going to clean up and do some scouting before bed, so if you wake up and I'm not here, don't panic."

I wouldn't panic. It would give me a chance to run.

CHAPTER 5

DESPITE MY RESOLUTE intention to sneak away, I slept like a rock. My dreams were like butterflies, colorful but fleeting. I woke groggy, surprised that it was still dark.

I pulled the blanket closer and shivered at the noise the wind made as it whistled past the tent. Somewhere in the distance I heard something howl. Did I really want to go out there again?

I couldn't stay here. I had to get past my fear and run before Malachi returned. I pulled my boots back on, cringing at the chill that came with them, then struggled into my heavy clothes and crept out of the tent.

This time it wasn't the cold that took my breath away.

My host had built up the fire, which popped and swirled in the wind. I could see him only in silhouette as he danced as freely as those flames.

He was barefoot and bare-chested, as if the dance made him immune to the elements. His hair was loose, and it moved around him like liquid silver, full of hot sparks as it reflected the fire. He moved as if he had joints or muscles where I didn't and was capable of controlling each one precisely.

He danced without music . . . or, no, that wasn't right. His dance *was* the music, and it made the night into music. His footfalls on the ground, the crackling of the fire, the whistling of the wind, and even the distant cries of wolves all created a song that I could only hear as one piece as his movements brought it all together.

When he turned and noticed me standing there, he stopped abruptly, and I heard a small sound of protest escape my lips. I had been utterly still, just watching, for several minutes. It hadn't occurred to me to sneak away while he wasn't looking. I hadn't even noticed I was cold.

"How do you do that?" I asked. "I've never seen anything like it." I had recognized some of the steps that Calysta had shown me, but watching her had never been that awe-inspiring.

"You were raised with every luxury." He was out of breath, and it made his sentences clipped. "You never struggled. Never questioned." The words came faster as he approached me, still speaking, his rhythmic voice holding me in place. "Never triumphed, or feared failure. You never hungered, or wondered if you would see tomorrow. You have never been asked to die for something, or someone." He paused inches away from me, close enough that I could see snow melt as it touched his bare skin. "The serpents' dance is a tapestry of passion and freedom and agony and need. You'll sooner find it in the trainers' lower cells than inside a stained-glass cage."

"I don't understand." I knew the meaning of every word coming out of his mouth, but what he was saying didn't seem to match his tone. The intensity in his voice was frightening.

He shook his head.

"I did a little research while you slept," Malachi explained. Whatever he had learned, he wasn't happy about it.

"I . . . see." If I ran, would he chase me? Probably. I wouldn't get far on the ground. On the other hand, he was a serpent. Snakes couldn't fly.

"I returned to your lovely cage and struck up a conversation with some of your fellow slaves," he continued. "They're not supposed to talk to anyone about you, but I can be very persuasive when I want to be. You're Vance Ehecatl. The Nahuatl name was Jeshickah's choice, but Brina didn't like how foreign it sounded, so she decided to call you Vance instead. It made her happy, so others didn't object, even though you are not technically hers. Brina's studio slaves didn't know *much* more than that, but what they were able to tell me was enough."

"Enough for what?"

"Enough that I can't let you go back there," Malachi said. "I'm sorry. You're just a boy, and I'm willing to bet that you have no idea how dangerous you could be."

"Pardon me?" Fight or flee? I didn't know how to fight, but I could probably surprise him and knock him far enough off balance to get a head start. I just needed to fly into the air, where he couldn't follow.

"If your freedom were the only thing at stake here, I would leave you to your naïveté, but Jeshickah has been trying to get someone like you for years. Quetzals are notoriously difficult to cage, but if she can keep you alive long enough, she will make you her weapon. I can't—"

Enough!

I shoved him as hard as I could. I drove my shoulder into his chest until he stumbled back, and then spun around and changed shape, beating my wings furiously. I darted through the brambly pine boughs, seeking open space so I could make the best use of my lead. It wouldn't take him long to come after me.

At the first break in the trees, I tried to gain altitude.

That was when the demon came from the sky.

It hit me before I knew it was there, driving my tiny bird's body down into the snow. My heart beat wildly, faster and faster, as I became aware that death was imminent in this beast's talons.

I changed back to human form, gasping, sputtering on snow. As soon as I did, the creature on top of me changed as well. Before I could get my bearings, Malachi had me pinned, with a knife at my throat.

"Even if your wings weren't stunted from a lifetime in a cage, a quetzal can't outfly a falcon." He stood and offered the hand that wasn't holding the knife to help me up.

I stood on my own and brushed the snow off my back. Now I had new bruises to go with the ones from Lady Brina and Lord Daryl.

"I thought you were a serpent," I said. Calysta said only serpents danced that way. Even Malachi had called it the serpents' dance.

"My mother was," Malachi answered. "My father was not."

"What's a falcon?" Other than a big bird I had never heard of til now.

"That's . . . a long answer. One you need to hear, but which I would rather give in the camp, next to the fire, than here. Do I need to truss you up and carry you, or will you walk without further dramatics?"

Forcing him to tie me up would ruin any chance of escape, so I said, "I'll walk."

"If you run, I will catch you. Do you believe that?"

I trusted it to be true for the moment, anyway. Now that I knew he could fly, I needed to come up with a better plan.

I nodded and followed him back to camp. Despite my less-than-willing mood, the fire gave a welcome warmth as I sat in front of it. Malachi sat on the ground, but I didn't let that fool me. He would be up in an instant if I ran.

"You asked what a falcon is," he said, his gaze lost in the crackling fire. "I assume you wanted to know more than the fact that falcons are large birds of prey, capable of hunting small animals and other birds. Though you *should* know that, because a natural falcon or hawk in this forest would think your quetzal form was a tasty snack. One of them would be fast enough to snap your neck before you could think about changing back to human form, so you need to be careful where you fly. As for the *un*natural falcons . . ."

He trailed off.

"My father's people are called the shm'Ahnmik. They are some of the most powerful magic-users in the modern world and one of the only empires that has *not* surrendered to Midnight's tyranny. Unfortunately, they see Midnight as an amusing convenience—a place to send the worst of their criminals—and not a threat, so they don't fight. Jeshickah would very much like to have falcon magic on her side, but the shm'Ahnmik are sensible enough to bind the power of anyone they exile."

"You thought before that I was a . . . a bloodwitch," I said, recalling the unfamiliar word. "Is that like the shm'Ahnmik?"

He nodded. "Your people are the Azteka. They're jaguar or quetzal shapeshifters. Not all of them have power, but the rare ones who do—the bloodwitches—are terrifying. As I understand it, the magic runs reliably in families, even when crossed with outsider blood. Jeshickah breeds horses, you see," he said. "She has for centuries. And she has no qualms about applying the same theories to people. In you she has a foundation stallion who has devastating power—a trait she wants—but a fragile constitution. All she needs is a dam who can introduce some hardier traits, and she can start breeding her own personal army, utterly loyal to her. We . . . I've lost you, haven't I?"

"Did you ever have me?" I asked. I had no idea what he was talking about, with stallions and dams and horse breeding. What I knew was that Mistress Jeshickah had taken me in when my blood family had abandoned me. She had given me a place to live and provided for all my needs. Malachi talked as if I should be afraid of what she might want, but if I ever had an opportunity to help the woman who had saved me, I would do so proudly.

"I'm talking to a boy raised in a box," Malachi grumbled, collapsing dramatically to stretch out on his back on the packed snow. "How could you even know what children or horses or armies are?"

Deciding that it would make my point in more ways than one, I answered, "I know what those things are. I grew up listening to Lady Brina tell stories."

He quirked a brow, clearly amused. "I have a hard time picturing Brina telling bedtime stories to a slave."

"I told you, I'm not a slave," I replied automatically.

"You have no idea what you are," Malachi responded. "It's clear that—"

"It's *clear* that you don't know Lady Brina very well," I interrupted. "Sometimes when she paints she gets lost in the colors and can't be distracted. Other times she likes to tell the myths that inspire her. Or she will show me a drawing, or a painting, and ask me if I can guess what has happened."

That was the magic of Lady Brina's work. She could paint one still image but hide within it the details of an entire story.

"I know her reputation as an artist," Malachi said. "I also know her reputation as a volatile, unpredictable task-mistress. When I found you earlier you were limping and had bruises on your face. Did she give you those, too?"

"You don't understand. Calysta—" My voice choked off.

Malachi's body tensed, and I remembered that he also knew her. "The slaves said she killed herself," he said, barely whispering.

"She destroyed the painting," I said, trying to explain.

"She *killed* herself," Malachi repeated, his voice gaining strength. "I heard it was quite a mess. Do you know what kind of madness it takes to drive a blade through your own wrist? So tell me, if your home was such a paradise, why would she do that?"

Why would she do that?

I stood up with a rush of breath, trying to rid myself of

the memory and of Malachi's question—the same question that had haunted me every time I thought about Calysta. Malachi was on his feet in a flash as well, but I wasn't trying to run from him. I wished I could run from my own mind.

"I don't *know*," I whispered. "Maybe it has to do with *you*. She told me not to trust you."

For a brief, horrible moment, I was certain it had *everything* to do with Malachi. Maybe she hadn't killed herself. Maybe he had killed her. But no, I had seen the tools, held in a death grip in her hands.

"Maybe it does have to do with me, since I used to know her," Malachi said, each word clipped and as sharp as a blade. "If she told you not to trust me, it's because she feared that I might tell you the truth about who she used to be and what they did to make her what she is—was. Sooner or later, Vance, you will find yourself in the same position, and it will destroy you, too. The woman you call Calysta used to be named Shiva, before she was taken from us and turned into a mindless creature who could be loaned out in order to clean painting supplies for a madwoman and teach the serpents' dance—a sacred ritual of freedom—to a caged bird."

I wanted to argue with him, but my tongue had turned to dust in my mouth. I knew there had to be a way to defend my world, but at that moment the pain of Calysta's death was too raw.

"Midnight is an empire that operates through slavery and fear," Malachi said. "You see, vampires are incredibly strong, and impossible to kill. They do not fear the elements, and they can transport themselves around the world in the blink of an eye. They have subdued most races, including the serpiente, the avians, the wolves . . . well, it would be a long list. The only reasons they have not conquered the entire world are that their numbers are few and they cannot perform magic on their own. They rely on spells that they can acquire only through the rare witches who are amoral enough to be hired out as mercenaries, which means they cannot fully subjugate those shapeshifter races that have powerful magic: the shm'Ahnmik, the Shantel, and the Azteka. That is why Jeshickah wants a witch, like you, who she can raise to be perfectly loyal and use to breed an army. I cannot allow that."

"Then . . . what will you do?" I asked as a chill passed through me that had nothing to do with the winter air.

"I *should* kill you," he answered. "It would be simplest, and safest. You could disappear in this forest and Midnight would never know who was responsible. But as it happens, I'm sick of having blood on my hands. I'm sick of making sacrifices for the good of—" He broke off mid-rant and swallowed thickly. "I want to bring you to the *pochteca*—the Azteka traders. They will know where you came from and whether you have magic. They are your family, Vance," he said, imploring. "Your *real* family. They are also the only people I know with the power to protect you if you agree to run."

My own kind, maybe even my own parents. I knew I should hate them for abandoning me. Why did my heart beat faster at the thought that I might get to see them?

"And if I *don't* agree to run?" I asked.

"The market itself belongs to Midnight," Malachi answered. "Any guard there will be able to bring you back to your . . . masters, if you wish. All I ask is your promise that you will speak to the pochteca first. Hear what they have to say."

"Then I can go home?" I believed him that the market would be a safe place for me; Mistress Jeshickah had mentioned Lady Brina going there, so it had to be part of Midnight. But if I was so dangerous, why would he risk letting me go?

"If you still want to." He put a hand on my shoulder to turn me and looked me straight in the eye, his expression so intense that I couldn't look away. "But I need to ask you for a favor."

It was on the tip of my tongue to say I didn't owe him any favors, but my mouth felt locked shut. All I could do was listen to his words.

"If we get separated and you go back to Taro, you will *not* tell him that I knew who you were. I recognized you as a quetzal and offered to take you with me to the pochteca. We didn't talk much, and I never learned anything more about you. Can you do that?"

"I can—" He looked away, and I broke off, feeling shaken. I rubbed my hands on my arms. "I don't lie to Taro. *Especially* for someone like you."

"I'm sorry," he said. "It will be okay."

"*Now* you're sorry? Why?"

"Because you're a child, and it's not right that you have so many people meddling with your mind." He looked through the trees and announced, "It will be light soon. We should pack up and get on our way. It's not far."

CHAPTER 6

MALACHI WAS A liar.

The market wasn't "not far." The market was *very* far.

We walked all morning, until my body hurt and I was hungry and tired and grumpy, and we still weren't there. I might have been grateful that Malachi didn't make me carry anything, like his heavy pack or the tightly rolled bundle that had once been his camp, but I suspected I was burden free because he considered me useless, not because he wanted to be nice.

When the sun was high enough in the sky to make the glistening snow blinding, I gave up.

"I'm starving," I announced. "I'm cold. My feet hurt. My legs hurt. My back hurts. Why aren't we there?"

Malachi looked at me incredulously. "First, you don't know what the word starving *means*," he said. "Second, we're not there yet because you lack the endurance to keep a reasonable pace in human form and the strength to cover any real distance by air. Third, I will accept that you are probably hungry, since you have the metabolism of a bird." He looked around for a moment and picked a mostly snow-free log to sit on. He slung his pack around and took out a tightly wrapped brick of *something* and a knife that looked sharp enough to make me step back. "We can't afford to stop for lunch—I don't want to risk getting there after dark—but you can eat this while we walk and it'll keep you going."

What he handed me then was a greasy-looking block that didn't seem to resemble anything I'd ever eaten. "What is it?" I asked.

"Food," he snapped before closing his eyes and drawing a deep breath. "It's called pemmican. The meat in this one is mostly rabbit. It also has berries and whatever else Torquil had on hand and felt like putting in this batch."

I still wasn't sure it was edible. "What's a Torquil?" I asked.

He started putting his belongings away again, ignoring the question long enough that I didn't think he was going to answer. At last he stood up and said without looking at me, "He's family. He's back home, and I haven't seen him in a while, because I've been here chasing my nightmares."

"Why would you chase a nightmare?"

Malachi sighed and shook his head. "Because the *rest* of my family is in those nightmares."

"I don't understand."

He was silent again for a long time, but this time it seemed thoughtful, as if he were trying to figure out how to explain. In the meantime he started walking again, and I followed.

"I have—had—a little brother. Shkei," he said, so quietly that I had to close the distance between us and walk lightly in order to hear. "He died . . . just a few days ago. I had a chance to save either him or my sister. I had to do something horrible, and even then I couldn't save both of them. Just one. I saved my sister. She's home now. I came back here because I wanted to be near my brother in his last days, but now I think I'm just not ready to go home and look my family in the eye."

I didn't know what to say to that. Before Calysta the worst loss I had ever suffered was one of the songbirds in my home. I had found it and cried over the still body. Taro had been the one to explain to me that animals had short lives, and that sometimes they needed to pass on.

It seemed silly, now, to care so much about such a little creature.

"How did he die?" I asked.

"In a cage with no windows," Malachi answered. "He died cold and hungry and in pain, far away from his family."

The answer, so flat and cruel, stopped me in my tracks. *"Why?"*

"Because the world outside your cage is harder than you could ever imagine," Malachi answered.

"Why am I still following you?" I shouted.

I wasn't expecting him to answer, but he did anyway. "Because you've never had to do anything for yourself or make a single important decision on your own. Trying to fight me and find your own way home would be too hard."

"You're the most arrogant person I have ever met," I grumbled.

Apparently that was funny. Malachi burst out laughing, so hard he had to stop and lean against a tree. Gasping, he said, "You spend your time with *trainers* and *Brina* and you think *I'm* arrogant?" He shook his head in awe. "Little quetzal, they have been so very careful with you."

"Lady Brina isn't arrogant. She's brilliant," I retorted. "And I don't know what a trainer is."

"Your crush is cute, but your taste is deplorable," Malachi commented. "Tell me, have you ever seen Lady Brina with blood on her hands? It tends to get in her hair, too, just like paint." He stayed leaning against the tree, but he was no longer laughing. Instead, his voice was savage. "As for the trainers, well, a trainer's job is to transform a free soul into a perfectly obedient slave. Taro, for example. They call him the gentleman trainer, because he can be oh-so-polite while he strips an individual of all hope and dignity.

He is careful and methodical, which I'm sure is why they assigned him to you."

"Stop! Just stop it, you *hypocrite*!" I shrieked. "You hate Midnight, and *Mistress* Jeshickah. I know that. You feel guilty about your brother and about whatever you did to save your sister. But that didn't stop you from flattering Lady Brina when you came to the greenhouse to trade. It didn't stop you from accepting her hospitality. If Midnight's so evil, why are you part of it?"

Malachi's brows lifted with surprise. "The quetzal is growing a spine, is he?"

"Stop that, too. You don't get to ridicule me. You don't know me. I just want to go home."

"And . . . you expect me to do what about that right now?" he asked lazily. All the energy he had put into his grief and then his anger seemed to have drained away, leaving a tired resignation. He had also evaded my question.

"You said you missed your family," I said, trying to reason with him. "Taro and Lady Brina are my family. I miss them. Why don't you understand that?"

"I do understand," he said quietly. "And I pity you. Come on, little bird. Walk with me a while longer, and then we'll go our separate ways."

I walked after him. I disagreed with many things Malachi said, but that didn't mean following him was worse than freezing to death. Besides, he was taking me to the Azteka. I didn't intend to stay with them, but it would be interesting to meet the people I was supposedly related to, whose myths I had heard from Lady Brina and seen in her works.

Unsurprisingly, we didn't talk much the rest of the way. I didn't want to hear anything else he might say, and apparently that was fine with him. Sometimes Malachi whistled or sang softly in a language I did not know, but at other times there was nothing but the sounds of the forest and our own footsteps.

It took a long time for me to dare to nibble at the food he had given me. It was as greasy as it looked, though the berries and meat gave it enough texture to be palatable.

A fine drizzle started to fall as the afternoon wore on, which suited my mood just fine. As the snowy brush parted abruptly to reveal a beaten path, Malachi said, "We're still a fair walk to the market, but I want some privacy for our conversation. Wait here for me."

I didn't say anything, but my expression must have spoken for me.

"Or don't," Malachi added. "You won't get far in the time I'm gone. If you go through the woods, you know you'll just wander, lost, until I find you again. If you follow the path, I'll find you even more easily."

With that he shifted shape and took to the skies.

I had little hope of actually escaping, but I still wasn't going to give up the first real chance I'd had. I returned to my quetzal form, but this time I didn't go higher than the tree line. At first I fluttered from tree to tree, following the road toward—I hoped—Midnight's market. I quickly realized that such a method of travel was even slower than going by foot, so I returned to human form and started out at a jog.

I came up short as a large, spotted beast emerged from the trees in front of me. I stumbled back, only to run into Malachi, who must have dropped down just behind me.

"It's okay," he whispered as the massive feline moved closer, then changed form. "She's one of the pochteca I mentioned."

As the woman who appeared in the jaguar's place looked up at me, my chest tightened. I knew that skin, that hair, those eyes. We didn't actually look *alike*, but the high cheekbones, the shape of the mouth . . . Except in the mirror, I had never seen such familiar features.

She must have noticed the resemblance, too, because she smiled warmly. She reached out, and I returned the gesture in kind. She didn't shake my hand but grabbed it instead and held it tightly as she spoke to me rapidly in a language I had never heard.

Malachi interrupted for me. "My friend doesn't speak Nahuatl," he said. "He says he was separated from his parents when he was young. I found him lost in the woods."

"Poor boy," she said in heavily accented English. "And I can sense power in you, too."

"That's what *he* said," I replied, trying in vain to take back my hand. "But I don't have magic."

67

"No, of course not, if you haven't been trained," the pochtecatl replied. "We are born either with or without the power, but we aren't born knowing it."

Malachi pulled me back, reaching forward to disconnect me from my overjoyed new would-be friend. "Vance, let me speak a minute."

Not likely, I thought. He had found this woman in the market. That meant she was more likely to be on my side than he was. I told the Azteka woman, "Don't trust him. He's kidnapped me. He threatened to—"

The sudden rage in her gaze as she looked up at Malachi was enough to silence me. He, on the other hand, quickly protested. "Yaretzi, I'm glad it's you. Your magic will show you I'm telling the truth. *They* had him. He ran away. They don't know yet where he is, or that we've seen him. If he's really a bloodwitch, you know we can't let them have him back."

"Are you mad, Obsidian?" Yaretzi demanded. "Boy, who do you belong to?"

"I don't *belong* to anyone," I protested. Why did everyone keep expecting me to be a slave?

"Vance," the pochtecatl said, "do you want to stay with Malachi or me, or do you want to go home?"

"I want to go home," I answered. I didn't need to think about it.

"Where is home?" she asked.

"Back with Lady Brina and Taro," I answered, even

though I knew the greenhouse probably wasn't an option. My attempt to travel through the woods had been a poorly planned disaster, but the reason I had left was still valid.

"Then come with me." Yaretzi grabbed my arm and started leading me up the road.

"You don't need to do this," Malachi hissed, pulling the pochtecatl away from me. "He's a kid."

"He's *theirs*," she snarled back. "I won't take that risk any more than you will."

"So you'll let Jeshickah keep a bloodwitch?" Malachi demanded.

"He's no more dangerous than the blind girl they keep, Itzli's spawn Celeste. This boy's probably just another one of that traitor's by-blows."

"I'm standing right here," I objected.

They both ignored me.

In a soft, pleading voice, Malachi said, "You know as well as I do that he will die in there."

Yaretzi didn't say anything else but instead started pulling my arm again. Her obvious anger intimidated me, but Malachi at least seemed to believe she was planning to take me back to the people I wanted to be with, so I didn't fight.

Malachi hurried behind us, grabbing her arm and trying to slow her down.

All three of us jerked to a stop as someone else pinned Malachi's wrists behind him. "Is this *Kateinas* giving you trouble?" the stranger asked Yaretzi.

Neither of us had a chance to reply before Malachi slammed his head back into the newcomer's chin, then whipped around, freeing himself. His hand darted toward the hilt of the knife at his waist—and then he froze.

"Go for it, Obsidian."

I was shocked to discover that the figure in front of us, dressed in fur-lined leather and a black, ankle-length cloak clasped with a silver brooch, was a woman with black hair and startling wine-red eyes. She was flanked by two men, both in strange uniforms that were nothing like the formal jackets I was used to, who carried short swords in their hands. All three of them were staring at Malachi with similar expressions of seething hatred.

"We're on Midnight's land, Hara," Malachi said. "If the guards see you with weapons bared—"

"It's funny, how you'll invoke their laws to protect yourself," the red-eyed woman answered, "even when it is obvious you were trying to break them moments before." She told Yaretzi, "I'm sorry if this creature has inconvenienced you. We can take him into custody if—"

Malachi didn't let her finish. Instead, he dove past the guards' blades, grabbed me, and started into the woods. When I tried to struggle, he warned, "They *will* kill you, if they realize what you are. Run. We need to get to the market."

I didn't have time to consider. Malachi's panic was infectious. I ran as if my feet had grown wings.

CHAPTER 7

A FEW IMPOSSIBLY long minutes later, we stumbled against a low stone wall. Malachi hoisted me up and over it. I was still struggling to regain my footing when he joined me, then sank down to the ground, panting . . . and, crazily, *laughing*.

"Been a while since I had a run like that," he said between gasps. "You've just nearly met the princess of the serpiente, Vance. Hara Kiesha Cobriana. She was probably on her way back from a delivery of tribute. Nothing more than bad luck we ran into her."

"She—" I had to stop, struggling to catch my own breath. "She doesn't like you any more than I do."

"She likes me a whole lot less," Malachi responded, with more cheer than the words seemed to deserve. "Given the excuse that she was coming to the aid of a merchant, she would happily have executed me."

"How many people want to kill you?" I asked as I looked around and tried to plan what to do next.

We were at the back of a small alley between two wooden stalls that backed up to the wall. Through the gap ahead of us, I could see people bustling back and forth, their faces down against the rain.

"Many," Malachi answered, "but the kings and queens of the great shapeshifter nations bow to Midnight. Starting a scuffle here in the market would be impeding trade, and in Midnight, there is no worse crime. That means we are safe here."

"That means *I'm* safe," I said. I stood up, half expecting Malachi to grab me, but he didn't. "Would she really have killed me?" I asked. "Or was that just a threat to get me running and save your own skin?"

He shrugged. "I don't have much respect for the so-called royals," he said, "but I do not believe even she is stupid enough to let a bloodwitch fall into Midnight hands."

"*You* did."

"I'm a sentimental fool," he said. "Also, after murdering Midnight's precious quetzal, they would have made sure to eliminate any witnesses—namely, again, me." Raising his voice, he shouted to a passerby, "You! Bloodtraitor!"

The man who turned, a scowl on his face, was dressed so similarly to the guards at the greenhouse that my heart simultaneously lifted with relief and clenched with guilt. The greatcoat I glimpsed beneath his heavy leather fur-lined cloak was the same deep burgundy color; even the trousers and boots were the same style. It was obviously a uniform.

"What are you up to, Obsidian?" the guard asked warily. He did not enter the alley but cast a cautious look about.

Malachi pushed himself to his feet and said in a heavy voice, "I believe I've found something of yours. Vance, this man can take you back to your—" He broke off and shook his head. "Back where you want to go."

The guard's eyes widened, and he looked closely at me before pushing my hood back. I winced as the rain started falling in my face but was gratified to hear him say, "If it isn't the quetzal. We were told to keep our eyes out for you." He turned and waved to a figure in the sky above. A large black bird fluttered to the ground and tilted its head, waiting. "Go tell Taro we have the quetzal," the guard told it.

Without even taking the time to return to human form and reply, the shapeshifter shot into the sky and continued to the north. If only I had strong wings like that, I could have skipped this entire misadventure! Instead, I was deliriously grateful that I would soon be home.

"Are you all right?" the guard asked me.

I nodded and stepped out of the alley as the guard

beckoned. I was exhausted and sore, and my heart still hadn't resumed a calm rate, but I was uninjured.

Around me the market was bustling with more people than I had ever imagined. They were set up in stalls and tents or just spread out on carpets with lean-to shelters keeping themselves and their wares dry. Most people weren't shouting, but the sheer number of them speaking at once gave the noise the power of a wave.

The merchandise I could see included brightly colored and shiny things that dazzled my eyes. Tapestries, jewelry, ceramics, fruit, jars and packages and boxes labeled with writing I couldn't read . . . there was so much here all at once. It was overwhelming.

Malachi exited the alley, which brought him closer to me and earned him a warning glance from the guard. "How did you get involved?"

"I found the kid lost in the woods," Malachi answered. "He said he wanted to go back to Taro, so I brought him here."

I shifted in place, struggling to keep warm now that I was no longer flushed with panic, and the guard's attention moved to me. The expression on his face softened. "Poor kid, you must be freezing. Here." He stripped off his own cloak, a thick piece with smooth leather on the outside and fur inside, and draped it over me. It was so heavy and long that I stooped under its weight, but I instantly felt warmer.

"Don't you need it?" I asked.

He shook his head. "I grew up wandering the Shantel forests," he answered. "I'm used to the cold."

"Shantel?" I asked.

"The third great magical civilization," Malachi chimed in bitterly. "The Shantel are leopard and mountain-lion shapeshifters. Some of their witches are as powerful as the shm'Ahnmik or Azteka." The names made my head spin. I knew witches existed, but I had never realized there were so many different *kinds*. Malachi continued. "Even Shantel without magic are brilliant warriors, hunters, trackers, or craftsmen. Except for a few, of course. The traitors who decide it would be easier to come out of the forest and work for Midnight."

"You're an odd person to call me a traitor," the guard replied blandly. He brushed my hair back out of my face and then twitched my hood up, covering my head and trapping out the cold.

"It is hard to learn loyalty in a cell," Malachi answered.

"Look, kid," the guard said, ignoring Malachi to speak to me. "I made my choice to take this job, for my own reasons. I know your story, but most of the 'shifters who are not already allied with Midnight do not. They will assume you're a traitor, just like I am. Don't let them catch you alone anywhere you might conveniently disappear. Okay?"

Given the number of people who had already threatened

me since I left the greenhouse, the warning seemed very clear.

"Vance, I'm sorry," Malachi said. "You're right. I am a hypocrite, and a coward. But I am trying to do the right thing by you."

"You don't know me." If the only thing I represented to this man was danger, why hadn't he just killed me in the woods, or left me to freeze to death on my own? Why had he risked taking me so close to the market? Why, if he was sure the serpiente would have killed me, hadn't he run and left me with them?

Malachi didn't seem interested in explaining, but he stayed nearby as the guard and I waited and watched the sun go down. Merchants diligently covered and packed up their possessions, some simply shutting their stalls and others loading wagons. Many cast sidelong glances at us as they worked, but they didn't say a word. Most were gone before Taro appeared.

My guardian greeted me with a warm smile, nodded an acknowledgment to the guard who had lingered nearby to keep an eye on me, and then turned to Malachi.

"Malachi Obsidian, you surprise me," Taro said. "I hadn't thought I would see you again so soon."

Malachi tensed and said, "I just can't seem to keep myself away."

"As long as Vance is safe, that's what matters," Taro said. "What are you asking for him?"

Malachi appeared cautious. "Since when do you offer to buy something that's already yours?"

"You misunderstand me. I'm offering a reward for his safe return."

"I have no claim to him," Malachi said carefully, as though he was worried he might say something wrong. "I just helped him do what he wanted to do."

"Very well, then. Enjoy your evening."

"At least I'll be more relaxed when I'm not traveling with a miniature volcano," Malachi said, clearly relieved now. "I guess it shouldn't surprise me that you wouldn't be afraid to keep an untrained bloodwitch on hand, but I'll sleep better without him. When he accidentally burns down Brina's greenhouse, I'm going to have a party."

Without another word he shifted into his falcon form and flew away, leaving me alone with Taro.

"What did he mean, miniature volcano?" I asked, hurt.

"Malachi Obsidian is a trifle mad. You shouldn't take anything he has said to you too seriously." Still, Taro sounded worried. "I'm glad he had the sense to keep you away from the pochteca while you were here."

"He brought me to the pochteca," I said. At Taro's startled look I opened my mouth to describe all the things Malachi had said, and how he had insisted on taking me to the pochteca and even suggested that they could take me away. What came out was, "Before I mentioned that I wanted to go back to you, I mean."

I clapped my mouth shut. Why had that lie, the one Malachi had asked me to tell, come to my lips instead of every defense I had intended? I didn't want Taro to think I had run away intentionally, or that I had ever *considered* leaving with my parents' people. That was all Malachi's idea.

"And what did the traders say to you?" Taro asked coolly.

I tried to recall so that I could answer honestly. "She seemed sad for me, because I had been separated from my mother and father. Do I really have magic?"

"You should. I haven't seen it manifest, but many powers only reach full strength in adulthood." He still sounded distant.

I wanted to complain about how Malachi had threatened me and said all sorts of horrible things about Midnight, but all I could bring myself to say was, "Malachi doesn't like Lady Brina, or Mistress Jeshickah. I was scared he might not help me if he knew I didn't think the same way."

"Wise," Taro said, some of the tension leaving his body, while the same amount entered mine.

Malachi bewitched me! He hadn't been asking for a *favor*. He had been placing some kind of spell on me. He had even apologized afterward for "messing with my mind," though I hadn't known what he was talking about at the time.

"You must be tired," Taro said, his voice finally gentle

once again. "If you want, you can change into your quetzal form and sleep while I carry you home."

It sounded like a nice suggestion, though part of me worried that he was offering to carry me because he thought I might run away again. I returned the guard's cloak with many thanks and then changed shape. Taro let me snuggle inside his cloak, where it was warm and I could tuck my head down and rest. The adventure of the last days had left me exhausted. When I finally got back to it, I wasn't sure I would ever want to leave my own safe bed again.

I had strange dreams while we traveled, and even stranger ones once Taro tucked me into bed. We weren't back at my home but somewhere Taro said was closer; it didn't matter, since there were dry clothes and warm soup and a large bed covered with a down-filled blanket.

I dreamed that I was watching Malachi dance. The movement was hypnotic. I tried, but I couldn't look away, even when he stopped and my gaze met his.

All I saw then were his sea-green and mist-blue eyes.

"Vance, there's something . . ."

His voice faded as a red wave swept between us, drowning those swirling eyes in a rush of heat and darkness. He surfaced several seconds later, but I had missed part of his message.

". . . you *need* to understand," he implored. "Vance, can you hear me? I can't . . ."

The world swirled again, the wave flowing by, backed

by a deep, echoing *bang* like thunder. When it cleared I saw desperation in Malachi's eyes.

"No matter what happens, please remember that I am trying to set you free," he said. "Survive. Don't give up. I will be—"

Silence woke me.

I didn't feel like I had slept a single second. My body was heavy, my eyes dry, and my mouth sticky. I would have rolled over and tried to rest longer, but the silence pressed in around me.

At home I could always hear birds, the whistle of the wind, or sometimes the patter of rain outside the glass walls of the greenhouse. Here . . .

I opened my eyes slowly, struggling to recall where I was and how I had arrived. My tired mind battled through the murk of exhaustion as I observed the down blanket on my bed; solid, painted walls instead of golden wood and colored glass; and faint, flickering light from a hooded oil lamp instead of sun- or moonlight.

I sat up carefully, my sore muscles trying to cajole me into lying back down for another six or seven weeks. I might have given in if the eerie silence hadn't made the spacious room seem claustrophobic.

I pushed the covers aside and put my bare feet on the plush rug that mostly covered an otherwise cold stone floor.

There were no windows, though that didn't mean the

walls were bare. I approached the paintings with excitement, thinking about the images I'd grown up around in Lady Brina's studio. One wall boasted a frigid landscape in which an icy river cut through a forest. The opposite wall showed the same scene at the height of summer.

They were pretty, but they weren't anywhere near as good as Lady Brina's work.

My interest in the art exhausted, I was shocked to discover that the door to my room wouldn't open. Locked? To protect me or contain me?

I tried another door and discovered an elaborate washroom with a claw-foot bathtub that had a drain in the bottom and pipes running toward it. I stared for several minutes, examining the mechanisms and remembering how much effort it had been to haul water from the stream whenever I wanted a bath at home.

Then I was back at the door that I hoped led *out.*

I rattled the knob, as if it might suddenly come unlocked.

The heavy wooden door swung inward instead, nearly striking me, and revealed a horrified-looking young woman in a long black dress. The gown was basic, practical, unlike the beautiful garments—works of art in their own right—that Lady Brina liked to wear. Around her throat was a simple black-leather band, perhaps an inch wide, fastened at the back.

In her hand was a small brass key.

"I'm sorry, sir," she said, ducking in a curtsy, her gaze on the floor as if she were afraid to look at me.

"It's . . . fine," I answered. She hadn't actually hit me. "What's your name?"

"Rose, sir," she replied in the same soft, deferential tones. "Master Taro wishes your presence. I am instructed to show you to him." She stepped back, opening the way to the hall beyond. "This way, sir."

As I followed her, a question came to mind. "Why are you calling me sir?"

Slaves in Lady Brina's manor had called Taro that, but never me.

"I'm sorry." Her gaze dropped again and her shoulders rounded, hunching in like those of an animal afraid of a blow. "Is there a different title you prefer?"

"No," I answered. It was on the tip of my tongue to tell her she could use my name, but what did I know of this place? Titles were a serious matter. I didn't want to get her in trouble if she knew something I didn't. "Sir is fine."

"Yes, sir."

I shook my head and tried to dispel my sense of unease. I was used to the idea of humans working for vampires and even assisting me as part of their duties, but Lady Brina's slaves had never shown me this level of deference.

Wherever I was now, the rules had changed.

CHAPTER 8

ROSE LED ME down a stone hallway decorated with elaborate murals. Carved hunting cats stalked in and out of wood paneling, above which the walls had been transformed into a fresco continuing the theme in shades of red, gold, and silver. Iron candelabra holding snow-white candles lit the hall, revealing unique carvings on every door and knob we passed. The entire *building* was art, down to the carpets beneath my feet.

We passed a half-dozen more doors, all closed, before the hallway ended and we were forced to turn left through an open archway. A guard stood by the doorway, but he nodded as Rose and I approached, granting wordless permission for us to pass.

Farther down this next hall, two men were speaking in low tones. I could sense that they were vampires, but neither looked familiar. I started to approach, curious, but paused as Rose sank to the ground a respectful distance away.

I didn't know *who* these men were, but I knew *what* they were, which meant Rose was right—we were supposed to show respect. Taro had given me permission not to kneel for him, and Lady Brina usually couldn't be bothered, but these two vampires were strangers. I watched them as discreetly as I could with my knees on the floor and my head bowed.

"I have to ask how you expect to break someone who can in fact boil your blood with a touch," one of the men was saying with a shake of his head. His skin was as dark as Taro's, but he was leaner, with black hair.

"The trick is not to let them touch you," answered the other man, whose long, dark hair reminded me of my own. Unlike his companion, whose jacket was as well cut as many of Lord Daryl's, the second man was dressed informally, in trousers and an unstarched shirt of such a deep russet that it was nearly black.

"We have company, Nathaniel." The second man turned to look in my direction, and his black gaze met mine, triggering the back-of-the-neck shiver that always alerted me to the presence of their kind.

"Be good, Jaguar," Nathaniel warned.

"I know the rules," Jaguar replied as he walked toward me.

Jaguar's Celeste. Mistress Jeshickah had referred to another quetzal who lived among vampires. I now realized she might be very near. I would love to meet her. Maybe she could be a friend, unlike the Azteca from the marketplace, who had hated me as soon as they found out who I was.

Jaguar caught my wrist, his grip strong enough to bruise as he lifted me to my feet and said, "You must be Vance."

"I . . ." All vampires had black eyes, but somehow Jaguar's were darker. Deeper. I swallowed thickly. "I'm sorry. I didn't mean to—"

"Nonsense, Vance," he interrupted. "I've been instructed to make sure you're happy and well taken care of. Jeshickah is very concerned for your well-being."

There was something so honey-sweet in those words that they seemed foul, like they could have flies or other things stuck to them. On the other hand, hearing that Mistress Jeshickah herself had expressed concern for me was almost exciting enough for me to overlook the fact that he had dropped her title.

I glanced over at the other man, Nathaniel, to see if he was angry that I had interrupted their conversation, but all I saw on his face was amusement. He shook his head but said nothing before he continued up the hall in the direction from which I had come.

"Thank you," I said. There, that was polite.

I tried to shake off the negative impression. Jaguar hadn't done anything mean to me. He hadn't said anything except that he was supposed to be taking care of me. He hadn't hit me or yelled at me, like Lord Daryl had done, or dragged me through snowy woods like Malachi.

"Rose, you are dismissed," Jaguar said to my guide. "I assume you were on your way to see Taro?"

"Yes, sir," I answered, instinctively falling into formality.

"Relax, boy. You and I don't need to use titles with each other," Jaguar said. "As it turns out, we're going to be spending a lot of time together. My mother was one of your parents' people, and Jeshickah seems to think that means you and I should . . . bond."

The last word had an ironic lilt to it, but a more pressing matter had my attention—a question more important than any other I could ask.

"Why do you call her Jeshickah?" I asked. "Taro told me I should never call her by name without her title. He never does. He says it's rude." It was also rude for me to question a vampire about anything . . . but I needed him to clarify before I could have any idea whether or not to trust him.

"*You* should never forget her title because you are a bird, and therefore nowhere near to being her equal," Jaguar answered. "Taro uses her title because he knows he is not her equal, either. No one really is. I frequently do not, because . . . well, I'm rude. Taro will agree."

The half smile on his face seemed very honest and almost elicited a matching reaction from me, before I squashed it. He rapped sharply on one of the elaborately carved doors, which was immediately opened by a thin man with a collared throat just like Rose. Another slave, I decided.

He half bowed to Jaguar, saying, "Master Taro is completing a project but will be with you momentarily. May I be of service while you wait?"

"Vance would like some breakfast," Jaguar replied. He hadn't consulted me first, but as soon as food was mentioned, my stomach rumbled, so I supposed he hadn't needed to. "Something simple."

"Yes, Master."

The slave slipped out of the door like a shadow, leaving us alone in a sitting room that—like all of the building I had seen so far—lacked windows. The furniture was hard wood, polished until it shone, and a tapestry woven of rich colors in abstract shapes warmed one stone wall. There was no fireplace, but there were runes above the main doorway that resembled those that warmed the stream in the greenhouse. Was this the kind of magic that Mistress Jeshickah thought I might be capable of? If I was, it would mean that people like Lady Brina wouldn't need to hire the unreliable cretins Lord Daryl complained about. On the other hand, why would people like Malachi feel so threatened if my magic was meant to be used for comfort and cosmetic things like this?

There were two other doors, but both were closed.

"Where are we?" I asked Jaguar.

"You don't know?" he asked. As if to himself he added, "I suppose you wouldn't. You've always been in Midnight, but now you're in Midnight *proper*, as some people call this building to distinguish it from all the lands and properties that make up Jeshickah's empire. Jeshickah had planned to bring you here soon, but the debacle with Obsidian and the market hastened our plans."

"So . . . I'm going to stay here?"

Twin emotions warred in me. Lady Brina didn't want me in her greenhouse; Mistress Jeshickah wanted me here. Was *she* here? Obviously Taro was. But this place was so different from what I was used to. There was no sunlight, no scent of fruit trees, no twittering of birds above.

"I had intended to tell the boy *gently*," Taro chastised Jaguar as he emerged from one of the back rooms. He shut the door firmly behind him and twisted a bolt to lock it in place.

"I think you underestimate him," Jaguar replied. "He doesn't seem to need coddling. Do you, Vance?"

Put in the middle of the two men, I wasn't sure how to respond. I wanted to agree with Jaguar, but I could see the disapproval on Taro's face already.

"Why Mistress Jeshickah thinks you will be a good influence is beyond me," Taro sighed, before turning to me. "Mistress Jeshickah thinks—"

"I've already informed the boy of Jeshickah's plans," Jaguar interrupted, with a sidelong glance at me that convinced me he was intentionally baiting Taro. "You can think of me as a confidant, Vance." He stretched out on one of the long sofas in Taro's sitting room, much to Taro's obvious annoyance. "For example, you can ask me all those pesky questions that our mutual friend here would say were presumptuous or offensive, like 'Why is the sky blue?' and 'Why does Mistress Jeshickah occasionally smell like a stable?'"

A startled laugh escaped from my throat. I clapped a hand over my mouth, only to realize that Jaguar was looking at me with a conspiratorial smile. Even Taro looked more resigned than horrified.

"The answer, by the way," Jaguar said, "is that Jeshickah is diligent about caring for her horses and does much of the work herself, despite having plenty of slaves to help. It is not wise to point the odor out to her, or to get between her and her bath. The woman does not tolerate filth, on herself or anyone around her."

This time I couldn't help but laugh—partly in horror, yes, but partly because I had never met anyone like Jaguar. Despite my first impressions, and my better judgment, I was starting to like this bold newcomer to my life. A confidant, he had called himself.

"Very well," Taro said, shaking his head. "Vance, you

are always welcome to visit me here if you have any questions that this irreverent fool isn't able to answer, but you are officially Jaguar's charge from here on."

Malachi's words about Taro came back to me unexpectedly, giving me a chill: *They call him the gentleman trainer, because he can be oh-so-polite while he strips an individual of all hope and dignity. He is careful and methodical, which I'm sure is why they assigned him to you.*

If Taro was the gentleman, what was Jaguar?

"Come, Vance," Jaguar said with a smile. "We should let Taro get back to his work, and I'll show you around the building."

I glanced at Taro, anxious at the idea of being sent away so abruptly, but he gave me a gentle smile and waved me off. "You'll be fine," he assured me. "You know where to find me if you need me."

The slave who had gone to get me breakfast returned just as we were walking out. Jaguar handed me a pastry from the tray and informed me that I could eat while we walked. The light fare wasn't filling the way the squirrel stew had been, but that was actually comforting. It meant no one was expecting me to trudge through snowy forests for hours.

"This is the west wing," he explained, gesturing to the hallway outside Taro's room. "All the doors on this side go to the trainers' apartments, so that is where you will find Taro, me, Jeshickah—if you were idiotic enough to visit her without being summoned—and others who are not so friendly."

"Like the man I saw you with earlier?" I asked, curious. "Nathaniel?"

"Nathaniel is a mercenary, not a trainer, but yes. You are young and impressionable and should ignore him at all costs, or else his morals are likely to corrupt you. *This*," he said, moving on smoothly to a door on the opposite side of the hallway, "goes to the courtyard. Do *not* go there. Jeshickah keeps a pet leopard, and it likes live food. This is . . . also none of your concern," he said as we passed the last door on that side of the hall, "because it will always be locked. This is a working building, Vance. You understand that some areas will be off limits, so that others may do their work, right?"

I nodded, wondering what work was done here. Jaguar had referred to himself, Taro, and Mistress Jeshickah as trainers—the same word Malachi had used with venomous hatred. I wondered how Jaguar would define his profession, but I was still too dazed by his glib narration of our journey and didn't feel able to summon big questions, much less understand their answers.

There was another archway at this end of the hall, and another guard, but the door was closed. "Beyond this," Jaguar said, gesturing to the door without opening it, "is the south wing, where the humans go about most of their tasks. You won't need to go there often, but if you ever need to find, say, the kitchen or the infirmary, this is where you should look. You don't strike me as the domestic sort, though."

"What *do* I . . . strike you as?" I asked. I knew how to tend Lady Brina's orchard and help her with her paints. I didn't know what kind of person that made me, especially in this world with no windows.

CHAPTER 9

"I THINK WE'LL find out what you are together," Jaguar answered. "As it happens, I remember being your age, and am of the opinion that a young man's full potential is rarely obvious at this point in his life."

Two responses warred in my mind. I wanted to agree with him, and promise that I *did* have value, no matter what Mistress Jeshickah thought she had seen. On the other hand, his words had also challenged one of the most fundamental facts in my knowledge.

"But . . . vampires don't age," I protested. That was an inarguable fact. They didn't age, and they couldn't die, so how could Jaguar possibly remember being my age?

"We aren't *born* vampires," he replied. "I told you before that my mother was Azteka, though she left my human father to raise me. Jeshickah chose me, gave me her blood, and made me a vampire centuries ago."

"Was *she* always a vampire?"

"As far as you and I are concerned, yes," Jaguar answered. "Rationally, she must have been born something else, but the mistress's history is another subject that is hazardous to one's health."

"I would never—" I broke off when I realized he wasn't mad at me for asking. I went back to another, safer subject anyway. "Why did your mother give you up?"

He looked at me, his expression suddenly serious. After a quiet moment he said, "That isn't the question you want to ask."

I took a deep, shaky breath. Every hint of irreverent humor had left the air. "Why did my mother give *me* up?"

"We don't know for sure," he said. "Azteka are strong, but they aren't immortal, and the world out there is harsh. Your mother may have been hurt or even killed. All we know is that we found you, apparently abandoned, in the woods. Did the pochteca tell you anything when you met her?"

"She was friendly at first," I said, "but when she realized where I came from, she . . ." I trailed off, remembering the way the Azteka woman had dragged me toward the market after I said I wanted to go home to Lady Brina and Taro. "Why were they so mean to me?"

"Vance, look around!" Jaguar said, sharply enough that I flinched. "What do you see?"

I obediently examined the hallway, though I wasn't sure what Jaguar's point was.

Thick, richly patterned carpet like I had seen throughout the building. White candles flickering in iron holders set into the walls. Magic runes etched discreetly into woodwork.

"You are warm and dry, safe, and have no fear of starvation," Jaguar said. "Your clothes are new, made of Chinese nankeen and tailored just for you. Take a moment and compare what you have to what you know of life in the outside world. Then *you* tell *me* why they hate you."

He leaned against the frescoed wall and waited for me to respond.

You were raised with every luxury, Malachi had told me when I asked about his dance. *You never struggled. Never questioned. Never triumphed, or feared failure. You never hungered, or wondered if you would see tomorrow.*

"You mean," I ventured, "that I have things other people don't have. They don't like me because they're jealous." I knew about jealousy, though I had never had much cause to feel it. Lady Brina's stories of the gods were full of jealousy, and the anger and warfare caused by it.

"That's part of it. The other part . . . How to explain? You're familiar with the serpiente, right? Your friend Calysta was a snake." Her name made me flinch, but Jaguar continued as if he hadn't just poked a raw wound. "Serpiente say they worship freedom. They don't think anyone should rule anyone else, except their own king. They use Midnight like a cautionary tale, a fable to scare children, but the reality is they *need* us. They use our markets to trade, and our laws to protect them from groups who might otherwise threaten them. They even use us to get rid of criminals who would otherwise be executed, because we can give them a second chance. That's how Calysta came to us."

"Calysta killed herself," I said softly, pointing out the flaw in that logic. What kind of "second chance" had we actually given her?

"Calysta was part of the Obsidian guild once," Jaguar elaborated. "I gather her suicide was preceded by a visit from Malachi. I don't know what relationship they had, or what memories seeing him may have brought up."

Another reason to dislike Malachi—as if I needed another one.

"So the serpiente trade with us, and send criminals to us, but they don't like us?" I said, trying to understand the bigger picture. I remembered how Hara, the serpiente princess, had acted, and that Malachi had told me she would kill me if she found out who I was.

"They feel that we take away their freedom to live and die as they choose." Jaguar's tone was nonjudgmental, as if he were leaving the final decision to me.

96

"And the Azteka feel the same way?" I asked.

He nodded, and added, "The Azteka homeland is far to the south of here, so we only see their traders—the pochteca. They have had unchallenged magical dominance for a very long time and do not like the fact that Midnight expects them to follow the same rules as everyone else."

I thought about everyone I had seen in the market. It seemed like a *lot* of people thought the same thing, judging by the looks I had received while waiting for Taro. "If we're doing the right thing," I asked, "then why do so many people hate us?"

"Maybe we're not," Jaguar answered with a shrug, as if the question were irrelevant. "That's something you will need to decide for yourself. You could be like Malachi Obsidian. He is welcome in these walls but chooses to live in the woods like an animal instead. He had his reasons to leave, just as I have my reasons to stay. His reasons, and my reasons, and those of people like Brina or the pochteca, may not be *your* reasons. You need to discover those on your own. Now come on. I want to show you something."

He started walking again, as if the previous conversation had been an inconsequential thing, easily brushed aside. I continued to ponder it while we stopped at my room and he instructed me to put on my heavy outdoor clothing and then led me through the broad front door of the building.

After so many hours inside without a single window, I blinked against the afternoon sunlight. Momentarily blinded, I tried not to stumble as Jaguar explained, "This is the only door in or out of Midnight. Spells keep my kind from appearing inside the building, so even we must go through this door if we wish to enter."

A wide path led from the building through the surrounding forest, but Jaguar did not lead us that way. Instead, he guided me down a smaller path, which brought us around the back of the stone edifice known as Midnight proper and to a large wood-and-stone construction.

All around us people were working busily—slaves, judging by the dull colors of their outerwear and the collars wrapping their necks. One was using a shovel to sprinkle gray ash over the path, which was slick with ice. Another was leading a beautiful horse.

The slave paused and half bowed, showing respect without relinquishing the bridle. I had seen horses in Lady Brina's paintings, but I had never realized they were so *big*! This one was a ruddy chestnut brown, with a sprinkling of white like snowflakes across its flanks.

"That's Dika," Jaguar said. At first I thought he was introducing me to the slave, but then I realized he was talking about the horse. "Jeshickah's Palouse lines are her pride and joy. Welcome to the stables, Vance. Lead the way, Felix," he added, prompting the slave leading Dika to continue escorting his charge inside.

"Felix is the stable marshal," Jaguar explained, "which makes him the highest-ranking slave in Midnight. He has permission to speak freely at any time and even give instructions to my kind or yours, when it is necessary for the performance of his duties." With a shake of his head, Jaguar added, "As you have probably gathered, every beast here is more precious to Jeshickah than you or I. Fortunately, they need exercise and company to stay healthy, so Jeshickah has given me permission to teach you to ride."

"*Me?*" I squeaked. Between my awe at just standing before these beautiful creatures and Jaguar's very clear description of Mistress Jeshickah's fondness for them, I hardly dared breathe in their presence.

"You don't want to spend your whole life at Midnight proper," Jaguar added. "Learning to ride will give you access to places like the market, or nearby properties like the di'Birgetta estate, should you need to visit there. If your lessons go well, perhaps you could even make it to Kendra's yuletide ball in a couple days—I see that interests you."

Sometimes I wished I were less transparent. "Could I really go?" I asked, my excitement almost eclipsing my nerves. Kendra's ball was *the* event of the year, attended by everyone who mattered in this world. I tried to picture myself among them, not as "little Vance" the quetzal or Lady Brina's greenhouse boy, but as a fellow guest. Someone Lady Brina might respect.

"Of course, if you choose. I'll speak to the tailor about having proper apparel made. But we're getting ahead of ourselves. Felix!" The slave looked up from his charge.

"Vance here is going to assist you for a while." To me he added, "Riding is a privilege that must be earned. No one touches Jeshickah's horses without knowing their proper care. Hard work will also put muscle on your bones and help you grow into your height. The next time Jeshickah sees you, she won't even recognize the scrawny, fragile child from the di'Birgetta greenhouse." He patted my shoulder hard enough to make me stumble. "Make us proud, Vance."

Yes. That was what I wanted. I would prove to Mistress Jeshickah that she was wrong. Maybe I could even convince Lady Brina that I wasn't useless clutter.

That was what I held on to as Felix put me through my paces.

He immediately put me to work on Dika, who needed to be dried off and cooled down after her recent ride. Every time I completed a task, he showed me a new one. Once Dika was happily stabled, my work had only just begun.

Weren't humans supposed to be *weak* compared to shapeshifters? Every slave in the stables seemed to be able to lift more than me and carry their burdens longer. When I paused in the middle of fetching water, trying to catch my breath, one of the slaves noticed my distress and took the heavy buckets from me with ease.

No wonder Mistress Jeshickah thought so little of me.

If Jaguar meant the day to be humbling, he succeeded, but I was determined to rise to the challenge. In the greenhouse I had never encountered a task that wasn't easy for me. Here, I had something to prove—*myself.*

At the end of the day, Felix assigned a slave to help me back to my room. I was so tired I could barely see straight, but I forced myself to bathe anyway. Mistress Jeshickah did not tolerate filth, and a day working in the stables had left me far from pristine. At last I collapsed on the bed, closed my eyes, and disappeared into the void of sleep.

I was alone in the forest, and I had lost the path. It was so dark I couldn't even see the hand I waved in front of my face. Snow swirled around me, driven by wailing winds.

As I struggled forward in the darkness, the slushy flakes became needle sharp. They pierced my clothing and my skin as they landed. Rivulets of hot blood trailed down my body, scalding me where they flowed over flesh and hissing when they fell into the snow at my feet.

My own violent shudder woke me. I jumped to my feet and turned up the lamp, needing light to dispel the darkness of the nightmare. I didn't know what hour it was, but I knew it would be a long time before I wanted to shut my eyes again.

When I opened the door, Rose looked up from where she had been kneeling just outside.

"Can I help you, sir?" she asked.

"No," I answered, "I'm fine. What time is it?"

"Nearly sunrise, sir."

It had been past midnight when I had returned from the stables. I knew I should sleep more, but I needed to clear that dream from my mind first.

I didn't want to go outside alone at night, and the walls here were too close for me to feel comfortable in my quetzal form, so I traveled the halls absently, stretching my legs.

Heavy strides took me toward what Jaguar called the west wing. I hoped to see a friendly face but doubted I would. I knew that vampires *could* be awake during the daytime, like Lady Brina when she was desperate to finish a painting, but most of them preferred to fall asleep at sunrise.

"Vance!"

Hearing my name spoken by one of the last voices I expected to hear caused me to whirl about. Malachi was standing in the middle of the hall, his silver hair and mostly white clothing making him stand out like a shining diamond.

"What are *you* doing here?" I demanded, bracing myself. Jaguar had said that Malachi was allowed to be here but that he chose *not* to be. *He had his reasons to leave, just as I have my reasons to stay.* I hadn't expected—or wanted—to see him again.

"Looking for you," Malachi answered. "I tried to talk to you in your dreamscape, but other magic pushed me away."

Good, I thought. "Last time I saw you, you threatened to kill me. Now you're following me. The last thing I want is you harassing me in my *dreams*!"

I glanced at the guards at each end of the hallway. Their eyes were on Malachi, too, but they hadn't jumped forward to throw him out.

"Actually, I saved your life."

"Either way, I have nothing to say to you."

"Then you can listen," Malachi said. "Even better, you can *look*. Come with me."

"I'm not going anywhere with you," I protested.

"You don't need to leave the building to see what I want to show you. We're just going to the east wing—have they shown you that yet?" Malachi asked almost politely, despite the hard look in his pale eyes.

"No." I hadn't even thought to wonder whether there *was* an east wing.

"I think you should see it," Malachi said. "*Then* we will talk."

He led the way. I remembered what Jaguar had said about this being a working building, and that there were some places I was not allowed to go because I would get in the way. I followed Malachi anyway, because I was curious now, and I knew Malachi couldn't hurt me or abduct me while guards watched from every exit.

CHAPTER 10

THE GUARD AT the end of the hall glared at Malachi but did not challenge his right to be there, or to open the heavy door that stood between the north wing and the east.

Beyond that door, the world changed.

Gone were the frescoed walls, the plush carpets, and the elaborate candelabra. Simple tin lanterns hung at intervals, bathing the gray stone in flickering light and illuminating open archways all along the left side of the hall.

"Take a minute. Look around," Malachi instructed me. His voice had gone soft and flat.

I approached one of the doorways and peered inside—then quickly looked away, because the men and women I saw there all seemed to be in the process of changing their clothes.

"Sunrise marks the change of shifts," Malachi explained. "They're readying themselves to work until sunset."

"What kind of work?" I asked.

Malachi shrugged. "Cooking, cleaning," he answered vaguely. "Some of them are skilled laborers—tailors, herbalists, and the like—but mostly the morning shift is responsible for the general drudgery required to keep a manor like this functioning."

"It needs to be done," I replied defensively. When I had lived at the greenhouse, I had helped maintain the grounds. There was no shame in working.

"Look here," he said, gesturing to one of the next rooms.

Inside, a woman was leaning over a small, railed crib. When she saw us peering in, she pulled the infant she had been holding to her chest, then knelt.

"Sirs," she murmured.

One child near her, a little girl with wide eyes, was old enough to stand and walk on her own. When she saw us, she didn't speak a word, but huddled near the kneeling woman.

"Go about your business," Malachi instructed. Shooing the toddling child away, the matron stood and set the infant down in its crib.

The woman's coarse brown hair, which was tied back with a piece of cloth, had strands of gray in it. There were lines around her eyes and mouth, her hands had a fragile, wrinkled quality to them as she bundled the infant, and the skin at her throat bunched loosely at the black collar that marked her status. She was barely my height and looked as if she might blow away in a strong wind, but her footfalls were heavy compared to those of anyone with a bird's hollow bones.

She repulsed me a little. I had never seen anyone like her. Was this what humans turned into when they got older?

"These children will grow up here," Malachi said to me. "Slaves from cradle to coffin. That's the expression, anyway. It would be a waste of time and land to give them coffins and bury them when a pyre is so much more efficient."

The small room was dim and gray, but the same runes that warmed the rest of the building glowed on the mantle. One child was sucking on a pacifier and another gripped a rattle; the broken rhythm it made as the child idly played with it was like rain.

"Do they go hungry?" I asked Malachi. It wasn't the question he expected, obviously. I couldn't imagine this fragile-looking woman or these infant children struggling in the harsh outside world that both Calysta and Malachi had described. When Malachi just blinked at me owlishly, I asked the old woman, "Are you cold, or hungry?"

She looked at me with a puzzled frown before she answered, "No, sir."

"What is your job here?"

"I tend the second generations until they are four, sir." When she saw the question still on my face, she elaborated. "I see that they are fed and kept clean, watch for illness, and teach them to mind their manners. I also speak to them, so they learn their language as well as a child of that age can."

"Notice she didn't mention playing with them," Malachi said under his breath.

"She's no different from the nanny who tended to me as a young child," I replied, indignant. "Taro wasn't always with me. I was taught to mind my manners, too."

"Can you really look at this and see *nothing* wrong with it?" Malachi demanded. "Most of these children will never see the sun. They will never *play*. They will never be free to decide what they want to do with their own minds, bodies, and souls. They will never be allowed to love, or . . ."

His voice trailed off and his fair skin paled even more as a woman with golden hair and eyes stepped lightly down the hallway. Her simple gown was made of rich velvet, and though she wore a collar around her throat, it was made of wine-red leather.

She stopped to speak to someone in one of the cells at the opposite end of the hall, her voice too soft to carry. When she turned to go, however, she caught sight of us.

Her eyes widened as she looked at Malachi, and her body tensed.

"Alasdair?" he called.

Without reply, she turned and fled, her bare feet sound-less on the stone floor.

Malachi collapsed, as if all the strength had gone out of him at once. His back struck the wall and he closed his eyes, taking a deep breath.

"I am not a good person, Vance," he said. "I have spent most of my life doing whatever I needed to do to survive from one day to the next. That's what *I* learned in these cells. You see, I was born here. I would have died here, too, if it hadn't been for a man named Farrell Obsidian, who decided a six-year-old child deserved a chance to live."

The words brought into focus why Malachi might be putting so much effort into me. He had been "rescued," and probably thought I deserved the same treatment. I could see the parallels; we were both shapeshifters, theoretically we both had magic, and we were both born in Midnight. Malachi had been taken away when he was six and had obviously been raised by someone who had filled his head with stories of Midnight's evil.

"I don't need rescuing," I said, trying to be patient with him now that I thought I understood his point of view.

"Yes, you do." He drew a deep breath and straightened his back. "The vampires don't know it yet, but they will never be able to make use of your power," he said. "That's what the pochteca told me in the market, and why they are willing to let Midnight keep you. That means Midnight has spent a lot of time and money on something it will not be able to get from you. I don't know what they will do once they know, but I doubt they will keep you in conditions as comfortable as those you are used to."

Malachi was genuinely *frightened* for me. As long as he didn't try to kidnap me again, I was determined to be kind—but firm. I challenged the logic of his statement, trying to convince him that he didn't need to worry for me. "As old and powerful as Midnight is, do you really think they wouldn't already know anything the pochteca could have told you?"

"Not this." Malachi shook his head sharply. "Most witches' power is essentially instinctive. They have it and will use it even if they never have any formal instruction. Midnight has never had a bloodwitch, so they have every reason to believe your magic works the same way. But the pochteca say that a bloodwitch is different. There is absolutely no way for you ever to use your magic unless you are trained by a blood relative."

"Then maybe I won't have magic," I said. "I don't *need* magic."

"A quetzal can't survive in a cage, Vance," Malachi reminded me. "What will you do when they decide you're not useful enough and toss you in one of these gray cells?"

The words made my stomach clench, but I said aloud, "I'm not human."

"Neither was the woman we saw a few minutes ago," he said. "The beautiful one with golden hair. She is a hawk, and she was royalty before she came here, and now she is a slave."

"How?" I asked. Jaguar said that Calysta had been a criminal before Midnight gave her a second chance. I wanted Alasdair's whole story before I jumped to conclusions about her.

"Alasdair was sold," Malachi answered. "Shapeshifters are born freeblood. That means Midnight isn't allowed to pick them up and make them slaves on an idle whim. A shapeshifter can only be enslaved if he or she is sold in by their own kind . . . or born in, of course, as I was. The child of a slave is a slave, even if that child is a falcon, or a bloodwitch."

"If shapeshifters can only be sold by their own kind, then it's *Alasdair's* kind who put her here," I argued. "You say I should blame the vampires and call them evil, but it seems like Midnight's laws would have protected Alasdair unless other shapeshifters thought she didn't deserve freedom. You told me before that the princess of the serpiente would like to get rid of *you* the same way. You lay evil at Midnight's feet, but you've made it clear that the world beyond Midnight's walls is no different."

"It's . . . Vance, it's *complicated*," he said.

"Jaguar says you're allowed to be here," I said. "If they were so evil, why would they let you speak freely?"

"Because I'm not stupid," Malachi retorted. "Midnight doesn't care if I speak my mind because they know I won't overstep the line. I will warn you, but I won't help you out of here, because a man who steals a slave or harbors a stolen slave loses his freeblood status. He *and* his kin are forfeit. I won't endanger my people that way.

"I just came here to tell you this: I *will* find a way to buy you out. Once Midnight realizes they cannot use your magic, you won't have any value beyond what they can sell you for. All you need to do is survive."

"I am not in danger!" I protested, the last of my patience gone. "And I'm not a slave. I keep telling you—"

"It's fine if you don't believe me now," Malachi said. "But when they give up on you, and you find yourself in a cage, and every fiber of your being says the only thing to do is to dash yourself against the bars until your body breaks, you will remember my words. Survive, and I will get you out."

"How noble."

I had been so focused on Malachi that I had completely missed the arrival of a strange man. I should have sensed him even if I hadn't seen him; he was a vampire, and a cranky one, by the look of it. He was wearing trousers, a half-buttoned shirt, and a scowl that would have made me cringe if it had been focused on me.

Instead, I knelt. Malachi snatched at my arm, and I had to slam an elbow into his rib cage before he would release me and let me do what I knew I was supposed to do. This wasn't Taro or Jaguar or anyone who had given me permission to be informal.

Out of the corner of my eye, I saw the nanny doing the same. She reached out to the toddling child and encouraged her to kneel as well as she could. The parallel between us was, suddenly, more disquieting than anything Malachi had said to me.

"Alasdair told you I was here?" Malachi asked the new vampire.

"She did," the vampire answered. "You frighten her."

"*I* frighten her," Malachi echoed. "So she runs to you, Gabriel? You're the one who—"

The vampire, Gabriel, took another step forward and Malachi broke off. His hand was clenched in a trembling fist at his side, but he didn't raise it.

"How is your sister faring these days?" Gabriel asked. His tone was courteous, but I could hear the sharp edge it held.

Malachi's body rocked as if from a blow. He didn't reply, except to turn stiffly and start toward the front of the building. He spoke not another word to me or the newcomer, who chuckled as Malachi fled.

I had forgotten until then the conversation I had had with Malachi about his family—specifically his brother, who had died "in a cell with no windows." One of these cells?

It was too late to ask now.

"And who do we have here?" Gabriel murmured as he reached down to tilt my chin up.

"Vance Ehecatl, sir," I answered. I bit back an explanation for my presence here. He hadn't asked for anything but my name, and as far as I knew I hadn't actually done anything wrong.

"Taro's and Jaguar's project," Gabriel replied, unsettlingly jovial. "Did Jeshickah's hybrid have an entertaining story to tell?"

I tilted my head, confused. It seemed that there were others besides Jaguar who were perfectly comfortable forgetting Mistress Jeshickah's title, even inside these walls. Beyond that, I wasn't sure what he was saying. "Sir?"

"Malachi," he said with an impatient sigh. "What did he say to you?"

Why? I wondered. *Do you want to make sure you can explain it all away?*

What had Malachi said, though? That shapeshifters could be slaves. That was something I wanted to think about, along with how I had felt when I realized that Malachi was standing tall while I knelt with the human slaves, but I didn't want to discuss any of that with this stranger.

"He said a lot of things," I answered. "Most of it was nonsense."

Liar! It was the first time I had ever looked one of *them* in the face and flat-out lied. I didn't agree with everything Malachi said, but none of it had been senseless.

I doubted that Gabriel believed me, but he let me go anyway.

"Stay out of the east wing," he said as he circled back toward the south. "There's nothing for you here."

I held my breath until he was gone. All around me I heard the cautious ruffling of slaves as they went about their business, freed of a vampire's presence.

I returned to my room and my bed, wondering if the stranger would report to Taro or Jaguar about the visit. If they brought it up, I decided, I would be honest. It would be interesting to learn more about Malachi. Had he really been born there, in one of those dim gray cells? If neither Taro nor Jaguar asked, however, I would keep the memory to myself. I could decide what to make of it on my own.

CHAPTER 11

DETERMINED TO PROVE both my independence and my competency to myself—and too restless to do anything else—I reported to Felix around noon, well before any of the vampires were awake for the day. I had done my best to sleep but finally decided it just wasn't to be. Refusing to let a night of poor sleep get the best of me, I threw myself into the work Felix assigned. I wasn't weak. I wasn't clutter. I was competent. I wasn't strong yet, but I could grow stronger.

At first the chores seemed menial, and I considered them nothing but a means to an end—a way to add muscle to my frame, as Jaguar had put it. I swept, then scooped ash onto patches of ice, before I was allowed near the horses. I reminded myself what Jaguar had said: even Mistress Jeshickah was willing to dirty herself with these essential tasks. Jaguar had been joking at the time—*Why does Jeshickah sometimes smell like a stable?*—but the words hung very seriously in my memory.

My diligence was rewarded. After a long hour of brushing, rubbing, and talking to Dika, "acquainting myself" with the horse, as Felix put it, I was finally allowed to saddle her and taught how to mount and dismount. I tried to strike up a conversation with Felix, but his attention never wandered from his task. He was constantly in motion, one eye on me so he could draw my attention to important details or make a rapid correction and the other continually roving the stables.

I was returning from my first loop around the corral when I heard a familiar voice. Even the bitter winter cold couldn't pierce my excitement as Lady Brina glanced back and saw me entering the stable, riding proudly.

She was riding sidesaddle, a style Felix had mentioned dismissively because Mistress Jeshickah did not favor it. The smart bodice and full skirts of her riding habit were what I would have expected from Lady Brina. I wouldn't have known what to do with myself if she had shown up in breeches like Mistress Jeshickah wore!

"Help me down," she said to her companions as I approached and dismounted, somewhat disappointed that she wasn't watching.

I looked around for Lord Daryl and was grateful that he wasn't with his sister this time; I knew I was likely to see that vampire again someday, given that I was living at the heart of Midnight, but I wasn't looking forward to it.

Today Lady Brina was traveling with a man I had never seen before, who had dark hair, tanned skin, and brilliant blue eyes ringed with gold. He surveyed his surroundings with the attention of a guard, but he wasn't wearing a uniform. The other individual with them was a boy a few years younger than me whose pallor contrasted sharply with the greenish-yellow bruises that lined the side of his face.

As soon as Lady Brina had landed softly on the ground, Felix approached her. He gave a low bow and asked, "Will your servants be tending to your horse, my lady, or shall I?"

With a familiar toss of her head, Lady Brina told the man with her, "Make sure my property is well tended. We can talk more later. Come, boy!"

The last command was to the child, who hurried after her.

I handed Dika's reins to Felix, whispered, "I'll be right back," and dared call, "Lady Brina!"

She paused and turned with an expression of grim annoyance that lightened when she saw who had spoken. "My quetzal!" she exclaimed as if recognizing me for the first time. "It was very rude of you to leave with no warning. As you can see, it has not been an easy task to replace you. Taro brought this one to me, but he is utterly unsuitable."

I looked at the bruised boy, whose eyes were downcast. Was that how she saw me? A replaceable servant? *Not servant—a replaceable slave,* I thought as I realized the boy was wearing one of the black collars I saw so often in this place.

I stared, dumbfounded. "Were you able to salvage the painting?" I asked, and then bit my tongue because she flinched, as I should have known she would. Was I *trying* to be hurtful? Where had those words come from?

One of the ever-silent slaves who tended the stables raced past us toward the main building. He didn't hesitate to bow, kneel, or in any way acknowledge Lady Brina, which was what warned me of trouble. I hurried back to Felix, who was beside Dika. The horse had seemed fine when I left, but now she was lying down and attempting to roll on her back.

Felix was talking to her in soft, calm tones as he reexamined her hooves and legs. The stranger had also knelt next to the horse and was rubbing her stomach gently.

"What happened to you?" Felix murmured to the horse. "You were perfectly well when you went out. Vance, did you see her eat anything unusual?"

I shook my head as I joined them on the floor, though I had no idea what I could possibly do. The stranger looked up at me sharply. Assessing.

"Who are you?" he asked. "Are you a guard?"

"I'm Vance. I'm . . ." I hesitated. His eyes reminded me of Malachi's. Not the color, but the intensity. The draw of those blue-and-gold orbs. I heard Mistress Jeshickah enter the stables, but it was difficult to turn my attention toward her.

Witch, I thought as I wrenched my gaze away.

"Who are you?" Mistress Jeshickah asked the witch.

"I'm the master of animals at the di'Birgetta estate," he answered. "I noticed this one ailing when I arrived with my lady."

Mistress Jeshickah knelt next to the horse and dropped her head. Long black tresses spread across Dika's side as the vampire leaned down to listen to the horse's labored breathing.

The stranger reached out, probably to touch the horse again, but . . . some instinct deep within me warned otherwise. Lady Brina might have been traveling with her "master of stables" if she was here to buy a horse or other relevant property, but why wouldn't she have introduced him to Felix in that case? Why would she walk off without him?

"Mistress!" I shouted in warning.

When Mistress Jeshickah lifted her head to glare at me, the stranger threw himself into motion. His raised hand barely missed her throat, then clamped on her forearm instead. His other hand suddenly held a knife.

The air became hot and seemed to shimmer. Mistress Jeshickah's teeth were clenched as the muscles in the arm gripped by the witch spasmed. She twisted, breaking his grasp, then wrenched his arm up behind his back and dragged him away from Dika. Felix ran to the horse the moment the others were clear.

Meanwhile, the witch staggered, then lashed out with one leg, his heel striking Mistress Jeshickah's knee, which sent both of them to the ground, entangled.

I cast my gaze about, searching desperately for anything that I could use as a weapon. I knew nothing about fighting, but standing there uselessly seemed worse.

My hand had just closed on the wooden handle of a pitchfork normally used to turn hay when I heard Mistress Jeshickah hiss in pain. I spun back toward her. The silver handle of the witch's knife was protruding from her back.

Nothing Malachi Obsidian had said mattered in that moment. Taro's manipulations, children being raised in cells in the east wing—*doubts* didn't matter, because this stranger was threatening the woman who had saved me from abandonment, who had given me a beautiful greenhouse and a life where I had never known fear or deprivation.

I flung myself toward the witch with a shriek that I never would have imagined coming from my own throat, and knocked the two apart.

Everywhere the witch's skin touched mine, I felt searing cold. I braced myself against it, expecting him to strike me down. Instead, his eyes widened, and he flung himself away from me with a curse.

What did I do? I wondered. *Did I use my magic?* Malachi had said that bloodwitches couldn't use their magic unless they were trained.

Maybe Malachi lied, I thought. *Or the Azteka did.*

Pushing my unexpected advantage, I moved toward the witch. He didn't know that *I* didn't know what I had done, or how to do it again. His eyes tracked me—which meant they weren't on Mistress Jeshickah when she struck.

She appeared behind him without warning, looped an arm around his throat, and *squeezed.* When he raised his hands to defend himself, she caught both his wrists in one hand. He struggled like a butterfly caught in a net.

Looking up toward the doorway, Mistress Jeshickah said, "Brina, please explain why you brought an assassin to my home."

Lady Brina was standing in the doorway, as she probably had been since the fight began less than a minute ago. She gathered herself and said with a huff, "We met on the road. We were going in the same direction, so he offered to escort me."

The witch *had* lied about being her stable master, just as I had suspected. I should have felt gratified that my instincts were right about him, but I barely had the energy.

Now that the fight was over, I became aware of the world around us. Horses shifted anxiously in their pens, letting out high-pitched whinnies of concern. Felix was in the process of tucking Dika safely into her stall; the horse had regained her feet and was tossing her head, fighting her handler.

"Very well," Mistress Jeshickah said. "Brina, go about your business and be grateful that I'm aware enough of your arrogant idiocy to believe your excuse. Vance." I jumped as she said my name, then froze, unsure if I should be kneeling. "Well done. I will consider an appropriate reward for your loyalty." The witch finally went limp in her arms. She dropped him into the straw, then snapped, "Felix!"

Now that the horses were settled, the stable marshal presented himself immediately and knelt in front of his mistress.

Though I had already seen the leather bullwhips that hung in the stables, I had accepted Felix's explanation that I would never need to use one—not on one of Mistress Jeshickah's prized, perfectly trained horses—and not asked further questions. So when Mistress Jeshickah lifted one from the wall, the last thing I expected her to do was flick the long, ropelike tool in Felix's direction.

With the speed of lightning and the sound of an accompanying thunderclap, the end of the snakelike weapon struck Felix once, twice, three times in the chest. Each time it struck his flesh, the skin ripped and blood gushed to the surface. Felix went rigid and a small, choked sound escaped his throat, but he made no move to defend himself or get away.

"What is the rule about strangers in my stables?" Mistress Jeshickah asked as she knelt to retrieve the witch's fallen knife. As she turned I saw the slice through the back of her bodice where the knife had penetrated. Blood had stained the cloth around the wound, though the skin now appeared to be solid.

"Strangers are not allowed in the stables," Felix replied. "I'm sorry, Mistress. I thought he was with Lady di'Birgetta, and I know I am not supposed to—"

"It isn't your job to *think*," Mistress Jeshickah interrupted. "It is your job to see that my orders are obeyed. Orders that exist to keep my property intact, and to keep things like *this* from happening. Is Dika all right, now that the witch's magic is broken?"

"Yes, Mistress."

"Is everything under control here?"

I turned to see Jaguar in the doorway. He briefly met my gaze, then looked to the witch on the floor, who had started to stir.

"Except for the ineptitude of my stable marshal, we're fine here," Mistress Jeshickah replied. She knelt next to the witch, pinioned his wrists again, and then pulled him to his feet. As she did so, I saw her previously injured knee start to buckle; she shifted her weight to compensate.

"Are you sure you're all right, Mistress?" I dared to ask, remembering how my blood had run hot when I had seen the knife in her back.

She tossed her head in much the same way the horses do when irritated. "Even magic does not slay us easily," she replied. But her skin looked paler than usual. "Jaguar, clean up this mess. I don't want the blood to attract rats."

CHAPTER 12

MISTRESS JESHICKAH SWEPT past us, pausing only to touch my hair with her free hand in a gesture of acknowledgment. After she left, I stood where I was for several moments, overwhelmed by my own churning emotions. Fear had become fury, then relief, and now . . . I didn't even *know*.

Felix hadn't moved except to drop his head so his gaze rested on the floor, where blood had fallen into the fresh straw.

I had seen Lady Brina's and Lord Daryl's tempers in the greenhouse, but Mistress Jeshickah hadn't seemed furious. She had been perfectly calm, just as she had been when the witch attacked her, as if she were attending to one more duty.

"Up," Jaguar said to Felix, who winced as Jaguar hauled him to his feet. "Are the horses safe?"

"Some of them may have panicked during the fight. I should check on—"

"*You* will do no such thing," Jaguar interrupted. "Who here is capable of doing your job?"

Felix pointed out another slave, who had been silently on his knees ever since Lady Brina had arrived.

"Fine. You, you're taking over as stable marshal until Mistress Jeshickah makes other arrangements." The selected slave immediately stood and began his rounds, as if nothing else had happened. As if the previous stable marshal were not still bleeding into the straw.

Jaguar dropped Felix, and he hit the ground hard, seeming to make no effort to protect himself from the fall. Then Jaguar looked at me. He must have seen my pale face and the unspoken questions in my mind, because he said to Felix, "I think Vance is concerned that Mistress Jeshickah's response may have been excessive. What do you think, Felix?"

Felix shuddered, still on the ground. "I disobeyed a clear order regarding how Mistress Jeshickah's stables must be managed, and in doing so directly enabled an assassination attempt that endangered not only my charges but Mistress Jeshickah herself. There is no possible response that I would consider excessive."

"Come here, Vance," Jaguar urged, "and tell me if you agree."

I crept closer, my own anger at Felix's carelessness warring with my reaction to the blood on his chest. My only experience of blood had been Calysta's, rotten and buzzing with flies. My breath came shallowly; I never wanted to smell that horror again.

"It's just a little blood," Jaguar said, apparently amused. "Nothing to be afraid of."

I forced myself to his side. Despite my fears I couldn't smell the blood at all over the aroma of the stables themselves. Unlike the congealed sludge that Calysta's blood had become, the trails on Felix's chest were bright red, seeping slowly. My eyes locked on those crimson streams, no longer aware of *Felix* or *Jaguar,* or even *Vance.*

Someone, something was whispering at the back of my mind. If I could only hear what it was saying . . .

The blood wasn't as hot as I had expected. It was—

What was I doing?

I wrenched my hand back from Felix's chest and my head up, prepared for Jaguar to demand an explanation, but saw his calm, contemplative face instead. "Do you think *I* am going to object to a little blood fascination?"

He had a point.

Before I could argue, he added, "Felix doesn't mind, either. Go with your instincts, little bloodwitch."

Perhaps I should have, but I had never considered the *name* of the magic I supposedly had. The word *blood* had only made me think if Calysta. I had never considered that, by avoiding it, I might be avoiding my own power.

I tried to summon back the little voice. What had it wanted me to do?

All I could think about was Malachi's warning: *What will you do when they decide you're not useful enough and toss you in one of these gray cells?* If I couldn't master my magic, was this what I would become? A slave who had failed to fulfill my one obligation?

I touched the blood on Felix's chest again, then glanced up at his face nervously. He was watching me calmly, no hint of fear, judgment, or pain in his gaze.

What was I supposed to do now?

Nothing; no response. Whatever instinct or power had been guiding me was gone now.

"I'm sorry," I said to Jaguar, dropping my hand with a sigh.

"We've learned something, anyway," he answered. "More experiments may be in order."

I tensed, fearing what those experiments might mean. More people hurt? More failure? I wasn't sure which scared me more.

"Vance, help Felix to the infirmary. I doubt Jeshickah will want him back in the stables, but I'm sure we can find use for him somewhere once he's well again. I'm going to double-check all the horses and feed before I go," Jaguar said, his tone all business once more, as if the strange interlude with the blood had never happened. "Come by my rooms tonight—no, I should make myself available tonight in case Jeshickah needs help with her new acquisition. Tomorrow morning, just before sunrise, would be better. There's something I want to test."

Test. I wasn't sure I liked that word. I nodded, though Jaguar had already turned away to join the new stable marshal as he checked on the horses.

As I approached, Felix pushed himself to his feet. I caught him as he swayed; his face was gray and his lips had a blue tinge. For a moment he hung on to my arm as if it were a life raft, but then his grip relaxed and he managed to stand unassisted. He had seemed so calm and composed earlier that it had been easy to ignore the fact that he was obviously severely injured.

"This way," I said.

I walked close beside him, ready to catch him if he fell or offer an arm to support him if he needed it. He never complained, but he took each step with exacting care, as if the ground might suddenly shift beneath him.

When we reached the infirmary, I pushed the door open and caught Felix's arm as he stumbled crossing the threshold. His skin was cool to the touch now; I wiped my hand on my pants instinctively once he had steadied himself again and I could let go.

My nose wrinkled at the sharp smell of herbs, which were set out on tables, hanging from the ceiling, and bubbling in pots on a stove. Human slaves hustled sound-lessly around the room, their brows furrowed in concentra-tion. The only voice I heard was that of one of the older healers, who was instructing a young boy in how to prepare a poultice designed to stave off blood poisoning.

She looked up from her work, saw Felix, and said to her charge, "Finish that. We're going to need it."

To me she said, "Are there any particular instructions, sir?"

I shook my head, not understanding the question. "Help him," I said.

"Yes, sir."

She took Felix's arm and guided him to a low stool. Neither of them spoke as she took a small dagger and cut down the side of his shirt, pulling the bloody garment away. Where the blood had stuck the fabric to his skin, it let loose with a squelching noise. Next, she grabbed a pair of twee-zers from the nearby table and began to matter-of-factly pluck loose threads and bits of fabric from the wounds. I had to look away as her ministrations caused more blood to gush from Felix's chest, but then I looked back, wondering how he could stay so still and silent through it all.

"The wounds are severe," the healer said, "and injuries suffered in the stables are prone to infection. Is he needed immediately?"

"No," I answered, remembering what Jaguar had said.

"In that case, may he stay here for a day or two?" she

asked. "If we can stave off fever, he should recover sufficiently to return to his regular duties."

"Do what you think is best," I said, backing away. I wished I had left earlier. *She* was the healer. Why was she deferring to me?

"Yes, sir," the healer said again.

I took another step back and ran into another slave, who had just darted into the room behind me. I had never realized how busy this place was.

It was time for me to get out of the way. Felix had been taken care of, and I was exhausted. I returned to my room with my mind swirling.

I couldn't get the image of Felix out of my head, but if *he* said Mistress Jeshickah's reaction was fair, why was I questioning it? At least here he was getting medical attention. How did I know he wouldn't have been treated worse outside? Malachi and Calysta had both described being frightened, starving, freezing in that world, but the slaves all around me here were well fed, well clothed, and healthy . . . except when they weren't, when they were in the infirmary.

Midnight wasn't a utopia—that was clear even to me— but I had no evidence that it was worse than the alternatives.

From these contemplations I slid into brutal dreams.

Snakes with crimson eyes like the serpiente princess in the marketplace swarmed from the ground, biting at my legs with needlelike fangs. When I tried to run, I was assaulted from the air.

Falcon talons as sharp as knives savaged my arms as I threw them up to protect my face.

Blinded by blood, I stumbled and fell. The birds of prey snatched at the snakes, bringing them into the sky for the kill. Venom and hot blood fell like rain, scalding my skin, filling my mouth and nose until it was impossible to breathe.

I sat up in bed, trembling and sure that very little time had passed. It was too early to meet Jaguar.

I walked brazenly through the east wing, ignoring the vampire who had warned me to stay away. The slaves I spoke with responded politely, but all seemed anxious to return to their duties once given permission. In the south wing I overheard snippets of conversations that fell silent as soon as I was noticed. If I had been one of them, they probably would have continued, but instead they were as mindful of me as I had always been of Lady Brina.

No wonder she thought of me as a slave. That was how I had presented myself.

I knocked on Jaguar's door hours early. If he was helping Mistress Jeshickah, I reasoned, he simply wouldn't answer. If he was free, however, maybe he could help me with my tangled thoughts.

It was not Jaguar who opened the door but a girl who looked a bit younger than I was, with dark brown hair, dark amber skin, and green-hazel eyes that didn't seem to quite focus on me.

Her head tilted as if she were listening to something very quiet, and she asked, "Can I help you?"

"Hi," I said. "I'm Vance. I need to speak to—" I broke off as I remembered that Mistress Jeshickah had talked to Taro about another quetzal when I was still living in the greenhouse. "Are you Celeste?"

"Yes?" she replied, her voice questioning.

The dress she was wearing was one I had come to know well. The material was finer, shades of cream and brown instead of faded black, but it was the same style as those worn by all the female slaves. Around her throat was a collar dyed a deep jade green with a fine gold buckle.

"You're a slave?" I asked.

Her expression never changed, but her body tensed. "Can I help you?" she asked again.

I shook my head. "How long have you been here? Where did you grow up?" The questions came pouring out. Why was she here, wearing a slave's collar, while I was . . .

I *was* free, wasn't I?

"I was born here." She added nothing more.

Born here. Like Malachi, who had also been a slave until Farrell Obsidian rescued him. Like me? They treated me well, but was that because I was free and respected, or because legends said a quetzal would not survive imprisonment? What better way to keep a bird content than never to let him see the bars of his cage?

"Master Jaguar isn't available at the moment," she added when I didn't respond.

"That's fine," I answered. "I can—I'll come back later."

"Very well, sir." She closed the door.

Am I a slave? They called me "sir." What am I?

Survive, and I will get you out, Malachi had promised. I had told him I didn't need to be saved, but what if he was right? Lady Brina obviously assumed I was property. What if Jaguar's "test" proved I really *couldn't* ever use my magic? What would happen to me then?

CHAPTER 13

"YOU LOOK TROUBLED," Jaguar said as soon as I stepped
into his sitting room.

About so many things, I thought, watching Celeste, who
was sitting across the room next to the hearth. Her head
was bent as she diligently worked to clean and oil a whip
that looked unnervingly similar to the one that had savaged
Felix's flesh.

"Am I a slave?" I asked, afraid to hear the answer.

Jaguar frowned, as if puzzled by my question. "Vance,
you're here of your own free will. I thought you knew that."

"So if I wanted to leave forever, what would happen?"
My voice rose as I challenged him.

"We wouldn't stop you," Jaguar answered. "If you
avoid starving, freezing, being mauled by a wild animal,

and being executed by other shapeshifters, you will probably have a short, brutal life, but that's your decision to make."

"What about her?" I asked, pointing to Celeste. "She's a quetzal, like me. Why is she a slave?"

"Celeste's father, Itzli, was exiled from the Azteka for heresy," Jaguar answered. "While in our employment he took advantage of a female slave. When Itzli realized she was carrying his child, he beat her nearly to death. Celeste was born blind as a result."

"She's a slave because she's blind?" I asked. Watching her now I realized it should have been obvious. Her eyes never quite focused on her work, but her fingers ran along the length of the weapon, working by touch.

"The Azteka wouldn't take her, because she was her father's daughter, so I claimed her as mine. I ensure that her needs are met, and in exchange she serves me. Now come with me. We have work to do."

"But what—" Jaguar was already through the door.

I wondered how long it would take him to come back if I refused to follow until he had answered all my questions. I didn't have the nerve to put the question to the test.

By the time I stepped into the next room, which was a bedroom at least twice as large as my own, Jaguar was already unlocking yet *another* door, this one black. When he pulled it open, I could tell it was thicker than most of the doors in Midnight. The lock was also heavier; I saw the iron key Jaguar used before placing it in his pocket. He carried a lamp with him as he entered.

"What are—" Once again I stopped before I could finish the question, because the room before me was unlike any I had ever seen.

I shivered as cool air washed over me. The chill seemed to seep up from the floor and walls, which were gray and white marble, polished to a glossy shine. The only visible furniture was a large trunk in one corner. The walls held no art, but they were not bare; black iron rings and hooks had been set into the back wall at inexplicable intervals. A wooden bar crossed the middle of the room, high enough that I would need to stretch my arms above my head to reach it.

This was not a good room.

"Jaguar . . ."

"Vance, meet Elisabeth," Jaguar said. He offered a hand to a woman sitting in the nearest corner, and she rose to her feet.

Elisabeth curtsied. "An honor to meet you, sir."

I offered my hand to shake hers. She accepted it, but her handshake was soft and tentative.

She had to be human. She wasn't wearing a collar, but her simple shiftlike gown was similar to the one most of the slaves wore. Her bare arms were marked with gooseflesh in response to the chill. I glanced down and saw that her feet were bare, as well.

"Aren't you cold?" I asked.

"I am fine," she replied. "Thank you for your concern, sir."

"Tell him about our plan, Elisabeth," Jaguar said. He turned his back to us and crossed to the trunk, which he opened without need of a key.

I couldn't see the contents from where I stood. I was more interested in Elisabeth anyway.

"Master Jaguar spoke to me about you," Elisabeth said. "He said the Azteka rely on blood sacrifice for their magic, and that it could help you explore your potential power if you had someone willing to assist. I am willing."

I didn't like where this was going.

"Absolutely not," I whispered, horrified. Out of the corner of my eye, I saw what Jaguar had retrieved from the trunk: a pair of knives, one all metal and one with a blade made of some kind of black stone.

Elisabeth's eyes widened. Her lips parted, her gaze dropped, and her shoulders hunched. She said, "I'm sorry. I didn't mean to offend you."

She looked devastated.

"I'm not offended," I assured her. "I just don't want to hurt you."

Malachi's words still echoed in my brain, but I forced myself to speak.

"Jaguar," I said, looking up at the vampire, who was

waiting by the trunk as if to give us privacy, "Malachi says I *can't* use my magic, that unless I'm taught by a relative I won't ever be able to reach it. There's no point in—"

"Something in you responded to Felix's blood," Jaguar said. "Jeshickah says you also demonstrated signs of power when the assassin attacked her. Do you really trust Malachi Obsidian—or the pochteca, for that matter—so much?"

Malachi didn't want Midnight to have a bloodwitch on their side; he would have plenty of motivation to lie about my supposed value.

"What if he's right? If I can't use my magic, what will happen to me?" I asked. "Will you throw me out? If I'm not a slave, then do I have any right to be here if you don't want me?"

"You *are* here," Jaguar answered. "We both know that Jeshickah hopes you have power, because that will help us in many ways, but she won't throw you out unless you decide to openly defy her. As I said before, this is a working building. Even if you don't have magic, I'm sure you'll find some way to earn your keep."

"Like a slave does?" This time my voice was less sure.

"Like we *all* do," he corrected. "I work. Taro works. Other shapeshifters work as guards, messengers, or artisans. You were born to privilege, Vance, and raised in luxury because Mistress Jeshickah thought that was best. But you should never assume that those who rule have fewer responsibilities than those who serve. Ruling the world is no idle occupation," he added with one of those quirky smiles that had first gained my trust.

He was so clear, so blunt. So honest? I tried to pick his words apart and examine them critically. Everything he said made sense. So why was I standing in a cell with a helpless woman, being offered a knife?

"I am not willing to harm someone just in case I *might* have magic," I asserted. "I don't need magic that badly."

"As I have already assured Elisabeth, you won't harm her," Jaguar replied. He sounded . . . *bored*. "This room has been scrubbed with lime, Elisabeth herself has recently bathed, and all my blades are regularly washed and heated. There is little chance of infection, and I will be here to make sure the wound itself is not large enough to cause damage."

"What if I just don't want to *hurt* her?" I demanded.

"Then you should know that a sharp blade, handled correctly, causes almost no pain." He held the metal knife out, handle toward me. It was small, the blade barely the size of my little finger.

"What about *her*?" I asked. "How do you suppose *she* feels about my cutting her up?"

"She volunteered. Ask her, if you don't believe me," Jaguar suggested.

I looked at Elisabeth. "You really want to do this?"

Her face lit up, as if I had offered her a prize. "Yes, I am willing."

That wasn't quite what I asked, was it? But since I wasn't the one offering to bleed, I felt silly standing there, objecting on grounds that were swiftly dissolving beneath me.

"Are you more afraid of hurting someone," Jaguar asked, "or of failing?"

The words needled me. They echoed my exact thoughts from earlier. Elisabeth was willing, and Jaguar had convinced me I wouldn't hurt her. Maybe I was only hesitating because I didn't want to face the fear of what would happen if nothing happened.

I accepted the knife and stepped forward. Elisabeth continued to watch me serenely, but I looked to Jaguar for guidance.

"The blade is sharp enough that you need very little pressure. I won't let you near anything vital until I know you can control how deep you cut," he assured me. "Here is safe, or here," he said, gesturing to an area on her shoulder and another on the back of her forearm.

Elisabeth held out her hand and set it trustingly in my free one. She wasn't trembling, but *I* was, which seemed bad when handling a knife. I took a deep breath, willing my body to calm. My first attempt at a cut on her forearm was barely a scratch. A pink line rose, with tiny beads of blood at one end, but that was all.

I looked into her eyes again, so calm, and then tried again, a little higher up the arm. This time a fine line of blood rose to the surface. Elisabeth didn't flinch or cry out, but I sucked in a breath, shocked by the vivid crimson line. The blood trembled in place but couldn't seem to escape its bounds.

Hypnotized by that shivering red mark, I moved farther up the arm and tried once more, with more confidence.

Flesh parted, and the blood flowed swiftly, a hot stream that splashed on the cold marble by my feet. Too vividly reminded of my dreams, I recoiled from Elisabeth as if she might be poison. As if her blood might burn. I didn't want to touch it.

"Vance—"

"I'm sorry," I said, dropping the blade. Elisabeth, who hadn't complained or uttered a single sound of pain, danced back as the knife clattered close to her bare feet. "I need . . . I need some air."

Jaguar sighed. "I'll take care of Elisabeth. We'll try again another day."

I hope not.

I fled to the stables. In the past I would have used my quetzal form to flee feelings like these, but there was no space large enough inside to fly, and outside the winter winds were too fierce for my unpracticed wings.

I needed to *move*, to push my muscles so hard I wouldn't have a chance to think. I forced myself to calm down and then saddled and mounted Dika. By the time I was done, the sun was just starting to rise, casting gray light on the path.

Why had I been so fascinated by Felix's blood that I was compelled to touch it? Why hadn't I been able to call that voice back when I was with Elisabeth? I couldn't believe I had *run*. What must Jaguar think of me? And Elisabeth? She hadn't complained. *I* was the one who had acted like a coward.

I felt Dika's balance shift, her front hoof sliding under her, and started from my reverie to realize she had drifted off the well-maintained path. We both tried to recover, but she slid to a knee. Then I was soaring, wingless, through the air—

I struck snow and ice, *hard*. My gloves tore, and sharp ice shredded my palms before my shoulder and cheek slammed into the ground. The coppery tang of blood filled my mouth.

I knew I needed to stand, to get Dika and make sure she was okay, but black and red shadows coiled at the corners of my dazed vision.

You're not that hurt, I told myself. *It's a scrape at most. You didn't break any bones.*

I tried to push myself up, but I was short of breath and shaking too hard.

I curled up in the snow instead. Maybe when the cold seeped in, it would numb my body and my mind.

Maybe it would finally let me rest. I closed my eyes.

I was in the greenhouse, but it was so much smaller than I remembered. A single orange tree, its trunk bent where it had tried

145

to grow too large for its enclosure, struggled to survive inside the glass walls.

Sweat ran into my eyes and down my back. The scraggly, wilted tree provided no shade.

The river will be cool, *I thought. I lowered my body into the crystal water. The white stones below me were slippery—and sharp, I discovered, as one cut my palm. Tendrils of blood flowed into the clear water as I picked the stone up.*

It wasn't a stone.

The skull stared at me with empty sockets.

I was lying on a bed of bones.

The water turned thick, hot. I clambered out as it began to scald my skin, and then looked back to discover that the whole stream had turned to blood. I choked on the metallic smell that rose to greet me as the water deepened, overflowing its banks and spattering my feet.

Where is the door?

There was no door.

I threw myself against the glass walls and heard a crystal laugh. I tried again, and again, until the glass shattered. Falling shards sliced into my body, severing flesh from bone.

Salvation came, in a way it had never come before. Pale hands reached forward, grabbed me, and dragged me out of my nightmare.

"Vance . . . what is going on?"

I looked up, in the middle of a dreamscape that looked like the inside of a bubble, to find Malachi standing before me. My gaze swept the iridescent vista warily. Through the bubble's flowing sides, I could see the blood and darkness of my nightmares swirling.

"Vance, talk to me," Malachi said.

"I want to wake up now," I replied.

"Vance, are you sick?" he asked. Malachi's concern made the bubble around us quiver. "Your mind isn't right, somehow, but it isn't what I normally find in the trainers, either."

"I can't get sick," I said. That was a human weakness.

"Apparently you can," Malachi said softly. "Maybe it's a quetzal problem I do not know about. I can ask the pochteca, if I can get them to talk to me about you. In the meantime, you—" He broke off, looking around as if he saw or heard something I did not. "Are you outside? Vance, why are you sleeping outside?"

Why indeed? I tried to remember.

"Vance, you're very cold," Malachi said. "I don't think your body is in good shape. You need to wake up and get somewhere warmer."

"I like it here."

Was I making any sense?

"Did you run away again?" he asked. "If you did, I will try to find you. If you didn't run away, I can tell them to look for you, and that you are not well."

"I didn't run away!" I shouted. He was always saying that!

The bubble quaked again. Nearby, parts of it began to shred, splitting like the skin of a rotten fruit.

Outside there was blood and screaming. Malachi's violet eyes went wide, and he put his body between me and the tidal wave of agony that rushed in from the bubble's wound.

CHAPTER 14

I WOKE, GAGGING, trembling, and struggling to breathe. My skin crawled. My muscles twitched. My head ached. And even though I felt like I was awake, all around me the shadows warped and stretched, threatening me.

"—is beyond what I—"

Burn! Must burn! The image of wildfire spreading across an endless plane forced its way into my vision.

"—can't you try—"

I was vaguely aware of figures leaning over me, but they were dim and colorless, fighting with the fire and the shadows, which seemed so much more vivid.

I lost my tenuous grasp on the real world and sank back into nightmares.

I woke again, this time on a little bed in an unfamiliar room that smelled of herbs, with an underlying odor of rotten blood. I knew that last scent too well. It was as if my dreams followed me, even when I opened my eyes.

I tried to push myself into a sitting position, but I was still too weak.

Just turning my head was enough to wind me. Once I had, I found that I was not alone.

Jaguar was standing in the doorway, his expression blank and unreadable. He was looking in my direction, but did not seem to be seeing *me*.

Sitting beside me was Yaretzi, the pochtecatl who had tried to drag me back to the market. She looked at me when I turned my head but did not meet my gaze before looking back down.

My arm was stretched out, extending past the edge of the bed. Yaretzi was holding my wrist just below two cuts in the skin of my forearm, which were dripping blood into a gold basin she held in her other hand.

"A bloodwitch is a holy vessel, dedicated to carrying Malinalxochitl's magic," she said, looking only at the flow of blood and the elaborate beaten-metal basin in which she gathered it. "When we come of age, we make sacrifice at the temple. Our kin make prayers on our behalf, and after that, Malinalxochitl hears us. We sacrifice our blood to her, and she allows us the use of her magic.

"This boy was never dedicated. Sacrifice *was* made; someone near him was bled, violently, probably fatally, and so his magic woke." *Calysta. Felix.* I had seen enough blood and violence to last me a lifetime, it seemed, but I didn't comment as she continued. "But the proper rites were not observed. The vessel was profaned. He does not give sacrifice, so the magic just builds within him, and he has no way to direct it. Without kin to guide him, he never will."

"What can you do?" Jaguar asked.

"I gave sacrifice with his blood," she answered. "That will quiet the magic for a little while." She put a hand over my hand. "Ehecatl, Malachi Obsidian tells me you were raised in this world and have never been given the opportunity to choose another. Now the vampires tell me that by their laws you are freeblood. So I will give you this one chance. I will speak on your behalf if you choose to leave here and join our people. Given your espoused loyalties you would not be allowed to study your magic, but you could have a place working in one of the lower households. Malinalxochitl's priests and priestesses will see that your magical needs are met."

"You would take one of your holy bloodwitches and make him a servant to your lowest caste?" Jaguar demanded, outraged. "And every few days, he will *graciously* be allowed to trek to the temple that should have been his birthright, so individuals who should have been his equals may bleed him?"

"It would save his life," Yaretzi replied flatly. "It is more than we would normally offer a traitor who has lived inside these walls."

"Does he just need to bleed?"

The question caused her gaze to shoot up and regard him with cold fury.

"I've never been a religious man," Jaguar commented as the silence stretched. "I'm not afraid of offending your goddess."

She stood, her back stiff. "I've done what I came here to do."

"So I'm right," Jaguar said as she pushed past him. "You don't want to admit it, but you don't dare lie to me, either. He doesn't need to become a slave in the Azteka empire in order to survive. He just needs to bleed."

"I am done here," she said again.

This time Jaguar moved out of the way, and Yaretzi left without another word or glance my way.

Sighing, Jaguar closed the door behind her. When he looked at me, his eyes once more held the kind sympathy I had grown used to from him recently. But I *had* seen that blank, uncaring expression earlier, hadn't I? Which one was real?

"You had a close call, Vance," he told me. "Our healers could do nothing for you. Malachi Obsidian somehow sensed your condition and brought the pochtecatl to us."

"I suppose I should thank him," I said. Once again the serpent-falcon crossbreed had come to my rescue. This time I had needed it.

"He seems to be laboring under the impression that

you are a slave," Jaguar remarked. "He keeps offering to buy you."

"He's fixated on me." I thought about Malachi, his odd obsession with me, and his warnings about what would happen once the vampires knew I would never be able to use my magic. "Do you believe the pochteca, that I can't ever use my magic?"

"Malachi's father's people said *he* would never have magic, either," Jaguar replied. "They said his father's magic was bound and could not be passed down, and that a half-breed falcon, or any falcon born outside their empire, would never survive infancy. Yet he seems to have survived, and if serpiente rumors are to be believed, the Obsidian guild started to demonstrate interesting magic once Malachi came of age."

"He was really born a slave?" I asked. He had told me as much, but I had scarcely considered it. A slave was a slave. It was hard to imagine one becoming anything different.

Jaguar nodded. "Farrell Obsidian, the man who leads that guild, bought Malachi when he was a child. It was apparently a good investment for him. I can understand why he now seeks to purchase you, too. With a bloodwitch's power on his side, he wouldn't need to fear serpiente law."

I frowned. It had never occurred to me that Malachi might be working on someone else's behalf. Could he be pointing the finger at Midnight and all the while wanting me for the exact same reason? "What is the Obsidian guild?" I asked.

"A band of serpiente outlaws," Jaguar replied. "We know them well here because the serpiente king considers Midnight a convenient place to dispose of criminals."

"Like Malachi's brother?" I asked.

Jaguar nodded.

"How did he die?" Had they—*we*, if I considered myself one of Midnight's people—killed him?

"Another slave killed him. The hawk. I believe you've seen her."

"*Why?*" I asked, with the same horror I had felt when Malachi had first told me of his brother's death.

"She's a bird. He's a snake. The two races were always at war. If it weren't for Midnight's laws keeping the peace on our lands now, the market would be total chaos." He took a deep breath and shook his head, as if frustrated. "But never mind all that. We need to think about what to do with *you*. Why didn't you tell me you were ill? The pochtecatl says you must have had symptoms for several days, if you were this far gone."

"I . . . there was so much going on," I said, but the excuse sounded feeble given the extreme results.

"It was a very irresponsible decision to go riding when you knew you were exhausted and distracted. In addition to your own safety, you're directly responsible for the loss of one of Mistress Jeshickah's prime breeding dams. By the time we found Dika, she had been limping on a fractured leg for hours. She wasn't salvageable."

"I'm . . . sorry." I whispered the words, because my throat had tightened.

"Don't waste your apologies on me," Jaguar replied. "As soon as you're well enough to walk, Jeshickah expects to see you."

Every beast here is more precious to Jeshickah than you or I.

Jeshickah has given me permission to teach you to ride.

She had trusted me with this privilege, and I had abused it. How many times had Felix warned me that horses responded to emotions, and I must never approach one unless I was calm? How many times had he cautioned me to keep my attention on my task?

I remembered Mistress Jeshickah kneeling in front of Dika, leaving herself open to the witch's attack, because she was so concerned with her beloved horse. Now my carelessness had led to its death. Would my punishment be any less severe than Felix's?

The makeshift sickroom turned out to be in one of the cabins where the other stable hands lived and did their work. Yaretzi, Jaguar explained, had refused to enter the main building no matter how sick I was.

Though it only took a few minutes, my heavy steps and nervous heart made the walk to Midnight proper, and then to Mistress Jeshickah's rooms, seem like it took days. Jaguar returned to his room and left me on my own. I was trembling by the time I knocked on the door.

A slave let me into Mistress Jeshickah's study and told me to wait. I stood in the middle of the elegant room, staring at the heavy black door on the opposite side. It was almost exactly like the one in Jaguar's rooms, and I suspected the same thing existed beyond it: a cell, like the one where Jaguar had run his "experiment" with Elisabeth.

When that door opened I sank to my knees.

The witch who had assaulted Mistress Jeshickah was chained against the wall, his tanned skin bruised and bloodied. *Why is he still here?* I wondered, trying not to stare. I had expected . . . I didn't know what I had expected her to do with him, after he had tried to take the life of the Mistress of Midnight. I didn't know what should be done with him.

"I don't have time for you right now," Mistress Jeshickah said bluntly, "so I will be brief, you will listen and obey, and then you will leave. Your carelessness cost me one of my favorite horses. My first inclination was to put you down as well, or at least grant Malachi's request to buy you, but Jaguar spoke on your behalf. He still thinks you have value, and I do still owe you a reward in exchange for your actions during the fight, so I will give you an opportunity to show your merit.

"You will take over the duties of the slave who is attending to Felix's tasks. Prove to me that you are worthy of my trust and my leniency, and your situation will improve. Fail me again, and your life will become far worse than you can imagine."

She turned her back on me and returned to the cell and the witch chained within. At the threshold she paused and glanced back over her shoulder.

"Or you could run," she said. "You are freeblood. Leave, and no one will chase you. You will also never be allowed to return."

When the door shut behind her, my breath flew out in a whoosh.

My skin was still intact. Yes, I had been demoted, but not permanently. She was giving me a chance.

Besides, where else could I go? To the Obsidian guild, which apparently wanted me for my power, so they could continue their fight with another king in another civilization? To the Azteka, who would let me serve them, forever a distrusted traitor, who was only allowed inside their walls out of pity? I would stay, and I would earn back Jaguar's trust and Mistress Jeshickah's.

CHAPTER 15

I THREW MYSELF into my work. I started my day with breakfast for myself and for the horses, then spent the hours until sundown brushing, washing, mucking, and sweeping.

In the next few days, I grew calluses on my fingers and muscles in my arms. I moved from my room in the north wing to a loft in the stables where Felix had previously lived. Others might think it was a step down in living quarters, but the wooden walls, soft breezes, and open air reminded me of my childhood in the greenhouse. One of the stable cats slept on my feet, and I once again woke to the music of songbirds greeting the dawn outside.

For the first time since I had left the greenhouse, the nightmares were gone, which meant that despite all the hard work I felt better than I had since coming to Midnight proper.

I saw Mistress Jeshickah whenever she took one of the horses out to ride. She rarely spoke to me directly, but I saw the approval in her gaze when she saw the attention I gave to my task. After the second day she gave me permission to ride again—short trips, when the horses needed to be exercised, but it was enough encouragement for me.

A little less than a week later, the blood nightmares returned. I knew the treatment for them was a simple one, and I contemplated pursuing it myself. There were plenty of sharp tools in the stables' workroom.

I didn't dare bleed there, though. Blood attracted rats and flies, both dangerous pests in a stable.

Besides, my blood had value. To the Azteka it was holy. Here, it was a gift I could give to those who had raised me. *Sacrifice,* I thought, *but not to the Azteka goddess Malinalxochitl.* I had seen Calysta give blood many times; Lady Brina had said that a shapeshifter's blood was powerful and inspiring, richer than a human's. Surely mine would be worth something.

I didn't dare approach Mistress Jeshickah, but I found the nerve to go to Jaguar. I wasn't worried about the blood donation itself. Calysta had always walked away fine—

Until she killed herself.

No. That hadn't had anything to do with Lady Brina feeding on her. Calysta had given blood on dozens of occasions, perhaps hundreds, in the time I had known her. I still didn't understand why she had killed herself. I thought it had something to do with Malachi and the painting. But it wasn't because of the blood.

But who was I to propose this to Jaguar?

A free man, I thought. If I were a slave, they would all know they could just take what they wanted. It was my right to offer—or refuse—as I chose.

"My blood has too much power," I said to Jaguar, my voice wavering just a little. "If I understand right, I could just take a knife and let the blood fall into the dirt somewhere and I would be fine. But I'd rather not waste it. Unless you think it should be so."

Jaguar didn't hesitate long. He pushed my hair gently off my throat, but the grip he used to hold me in place was harder than it needed to be. I wasn't going to try to escape.

Unless it hurt?

I tensed and tried to brace myself, thinking that even if it *did* hurt I wouldn't struggle.

There was a pinching feeling at my throat at first, but that went away quickly. The bite itself grew numb, though a tingling sensation spread across the rest of my body. I had to fight to keep still, not because I was in pain, but because it *tickled*, especially in places like my wrists, where I normally felt my pulse. I wanted to scratch at that spot, but Jaguar was holding on to my arms in a way that kept me from doing so.

Jaguar often laughed, but after he pulled back I heard him giggle for the first time.

He dropped me negligently, so that I nearly fell, and I almost objected before he stumbled back and his shoulders hit the wall with a thud. With his eyes closed and his head bowed, he bit his lip and took a deep breath, as if he were struggling to control himself.

Then he giggled again and slid down until he was sitting on the floor.

Dizzy, I decided I would join him, but he waved me away.

"No, go," he said. "Get out of here, or I'll take too much. You . . ." He trailed off and shook his head. "I guess you might be worth keeping around after all. Go, go, go. Wait. Go to the kitchens. You should eat something. They'll know what to give you. Then lie down for a while. Don't go back to work today. I took more than I should have."

He didn't seem worried, just cautious, so only one thought crossed my mind after all those instructions: *Free time?* Apparently I had done something right.

I stumbled and slid my way down to the kitchens, fighting occasional spells of dizziness. Despite my excitement for free time, I ended up eating and drinking what they gave me mechanically. I didn't have the energy to go back to my room above the stables, so I let them put me to bed in one of the vacant cots in the east wing.

If I had dreams, they disappeared into the mist when I opened my eyes.

I was still a little groggy when I woke, and very thirsty, but the nameless, voiceless humans who lingered around me provided everything I wanted before I even asked for it. Once I felt capable of walking, and my attendants declared it safe for me to do so, I wasn't sure where to go.

What did I want to do? In the greenhouse as well as here, I hadn't ever had many hobbies beyond my chores. I didn't dare ride, not when my head still felt a little floaty if I moved too fast.

I should check on Felix, I decided, *and Elisabeth.*

I wasn't sure where to find Felix, so I started in the infirmary. They would know when he had been released, and might know where he had gone to work. Barefoot and wild-haired, I padded down the hall.

It was midday, a time when most vampires slept, and even the infirmary was quiet. There was one sleepy-eyed slave present, who greeted me with a nod and a "sir," but otherwise the main room was empty. The bloody water and cloths used to wash Felix's wounds had been cleaned up, and all the herbs, poultices, and salves were arranged neatly on the shelves. Where there had been anxiety and carnage, I now found sterile stillness, as if the previous week's violence had never happened.

The next room was starkly utilitarian, like the cells in

the east wing. Gray stone walls and floor, with six cots, half of which were currently occupied. The blankets atop them were gray-brown, practical things, without embroidery or quilting.

Three people looked up at me the moment I stepped through the door.

The first was a boy, probably several years younger than me. From brow to jaw, one side of his face was livid indigo and cranberry, dark bruises that had swollen one of his eyes mostly shut.

Did he fall? I wondered. *Or did someone do this to him?*

The second cot held a woman. She wasn't *old,* but she had fine lines at the sides of her mouth and on her brow. Her face was flushed, and she had pushed the blanket off her shoulders.

Felix was in the third cot. When I looked at him, he said something, but the words were meaningless to me.

I leaned close, trying to make sense of the whispered sounds.

"Te extraño, niña."

If he was speaking any language but gibberish, I didn't recognize it.

I could feel the heat rising off his body, and my nose caught the rank smell of sweat and decay. It brought back the memory of the scalding river in my nightmare. I reeled and retreated to the main infirmary room. I asked the slave there, "Will Felix be all right?"

"I'm sorry, sir, but it's unlikely," he replied. "He rallied for a little while, but then the infection took hold. Mistress Jeshickah has approved the best medicines for him, but we cannot seem to clear the blood poisoning."

It had been more than a week. Had he been here all this time?

"What happened to the other two?" I asked in a daze.

"The woman has childbed fever," he answered, "but I believe she will recover soon. The boy was impertinent with Lord Daryl."

I realized then that I had seen the boy before. He had come and gone with Lady Brina, and the bruises he wore now were newer versions of the ones I had seen then. I wondered how Lord Daryl defined "impertinent," and whether the boy's trespass had been any more severe than my own.

As serious as Felix's?

Felix himself had agreed that his punishment was appropriate. If *he* didn't complain, who was I to question?

Te extraño, niña.

I shook my head. I didn't know what those words meant, if they were even words, but they haunted me. What about Elisabeth? Jaguar had assured me that she would be fine, but I needed to know.

I tried unsuccessfully to turn the doorknob before I decided to knock instead. I let my knuckles rap gently against the dark wood paneling a couple of times before it occurred to me that Jaguar was probably asleep at this hour.

Celeste opened the door. Her hair was rumpled, and the long, heavy dress she was wearing was made of soft, thick cotton, suitable for a nightgown. I had woken her, too.

"Can I help you?" she asked.

"I'm sorry," I said. "I wanted to speak to Jaguar."

Jaguar stepped up behind Celeste. He whispered something to her, and she retreated into the room. Jaguar yawned and said, "Vance. Are you unwell?"

"N-no," I stammered. "I didn't mean to disturb you. I wanted to check on Elisabeth. Felix is very ill. I just . . ." I trailed off.

"Elisabeth is fine, just as I assured you she would be," Jaguar answered. "As for Felix, no matter how diligent the hands are, stables are never sterile. The whip that tore Felix's flesh had been hanging there for weeks, unused, but exposed to all the pestilence that exists in such a place. The healers will do what they can, but if he is still ill after this much time, you should prepare yourself."

"You think he'll die?"

"That's what humans *do*," Jaguar replied. "They're not immortal. They die from sickness, from frailty, from age. They accept their deaths as inevitable, and so must you." His words were even blunter than usual, probably because he obviously wanted to go back to bed. "I will let Elisabeth know of your concern and send her to see you later. Now go away."

The door shut in my face.

I didn't want to go back to bed, but my body didn't seem able to stay up, either. I was simultaneously restless and exhausted. I went to my room to sleep a little longer, but by late afternoon I couldn't resist the pull of the horses downstairs or of the work I knew still needed to get done.

The first time I reached up to take down one of the heavy saddles, my vision blackened and my knees buckled. I sat down abruptly on the floor and put my head between my legs. Just a lingering effect of blood loss? Or something worse?

The dizzy spell passed and I looked up to find one of the stable hands standing over me. He informed me that Jaguar had assigned him to keep an eye on me if I came back to the stables, and explained that I should sit and wait, since someone had already gone to fetch him. I didn't have a chance to protest that Jaguar was sleeping and I didn't want to bother him.

Instead of Jaguar it was Taro who came to pull me gently to my feet. I braced myself for another scathing, disappointed talk from my old guardian, like the one I'd had with Jaguar when I first woke from my accident. I hadn't seen my old guardian since he had turned me over to Jaguar's care. Now he looked down to where I sat with my butt in the straw.

Tone gentle, he said, "He shouldn't have let you come back to work so soon. Come, Vance. I'll have someone replace you."

I stood and then swayed; the movement had been too quick, in my condition. Taro responded by picking me up.

"You're in bad shape, dear quetzal," he said. "If it weren't for your shapeshifter's constitution, you would still be unconscious, or worse. Relax for a few days. I will speak to Mistress Jeshickah, and if it is in your best interests to let you become a bleeder, we will adjust your work schedule accordingly."

"I saw people leave the greenhouse after Lady Brina fed," I said. "Even the humans were in better shape than I am now."

"Lady Brina apparently has better restraint than our Jaguar," Taro said dryly. "Also, we normally do not have children donate. Azteka or not, you are still only fourteen. We need to balance the needs of your power with the limitations of your body."

CHAPTER 16

BY THE NEXT day I felt well enough to attend to some of the lighter chores in the stables. The slaves there told me I had been excused from that work, but I enjoyed finding tasks to busy my hands and mind.

As Jaguar had promised, Elisabeth came to see me.

"Master Jaguar told me that I should visit you and let you know that I am at your disposal. Anything you wish I shall do my best to provide. I am also to explain that his time may be more limited for a while as he is occupied with a new project."

"What kind of project?" I asked.

She shook her head. "I'm sorry, sir. I do not know."

I wasn't sure what I was supposed to do with her. Was this some test of Jaguar's, to see what I would do with responsibility? She was wearing a slave's collar now, I noticed.

When I asked why she hadn't been when I first saw her, she informed me that she hadn't earned it yet then.

"What does that mean?"

"I don't know how to answer that," she answered. "I'm sorry." She dropped her gaze.

"It means she's proven herself," volunteered one of the shapeshifter guards, who had come in a few minutes ago and was now brushing down his horse. "That's what the trainers mean when they say a 'project,'" he added. "It means someone was sold to them, and they're working on teaching that person his or her place. No one really knows what goes on in a trainer's cell, except the trainers and the slaves, of course. For folk like us it's better not to give it too much thought."

He thinks I'm one of them, I thought. The guard was speaking to me, shapeshifter to shapeshifter. Or bloodtraitor to bloodtraitor, as outsiders would call us.

Well, I *was* one of them, wasn't I? The Azteka hadn't offered me a glamorous life, but they had offered me a life. The Obsidian guild might only want me for my power, but they were supposedly "my own kind," shapeshifters with whom I could have allied myself.

"What does that mean, for a slave to prove herself?" I asked.

The guard shrugged. "Well, the way trainers talk about them, a broken slave is like a work of art. She reflects on the one who made her." He nodded to Elisabeth. "He wouldn't let her go out in a collar unless he trusted her to show well."

I looked at Elisabeth, about to apologize for speaking about her so impersonally, but the expression she wore was the same placid, accepting one she had in the cell when she said she was willing to let me bleed her.

Was that how she proved herself? I wondered.

My head was spinning, and it wasn't from blood loss.

It was another three days before I felt ready, but as soon as I was sure I could do so safely, I rode out to the market. The blood dreams had started again the night before, but they weren't bad enough yet to exhaust me and destroy my ability to function. I needed to have my questions answered by someone *other* than the trainers.

I wanted to speak to the pochteca.

No luck. The stall belonging to the pochteca was closed. I was staring at it forlornly when the Shantel guard who had taken care of me last time I was there stepped up beside me.

"Are you all right?" he asked.

I nodded. "I wanted to ask them something."

"Is it something I might be able to answer for you?" he asked. "The pochteca should return in a few weeks, but they rarely answer questions from anyone they see as belonging to Midnight."

"Why do so many people hate Midnight?" I asked. I

knew what Malachi had said, and what Jaguar had said. This man was allied with Midnight, but he was still a shapeshifter, and he saw the goings-on in the market every day. I wanted to hear every answer I could get, every point of view.

Guard or not, he answered immediately. "Because the vampires are in charge, and they're brutal about their rule."

"Then why do *you* work for them?"

"I'm not sure there's a better option," he answered. "If you're thinking about running, kid, you should make sure you know where you intend to go. The Azteka might be willing to put you out of your misery, but they will never trust that you aren't loyal to Midnight. The Shantel—my people—execute traitors like us on sight. The other shape-shifter nations would sell you back in a heartbeat to avoid an inconvenient moral dilemma. They all say they hate Midnight, but there's a reason no one has really stood up against the vampires' empire. They're afraid of what the world might be like without it."

"I'm worried that they've been lying to me," I said softly. "Manipulating me."

"Assuming they have been," the guard replied, "what does that change?"

"It changes . . ." I trailed off. "How can I trust them?"

"Trust them or don't. Does it matter?" he asked. "Sure, not everyone in this world is going to love you for liv-ing with the lords and ladies of Midnight, but does that mean you're willing to give it all up? I suggest you think it through before you commit to a life of hardship."

"Thanks for the advice," I said, defeated. It wasn't the first time he had helped me, or warned me, but suddenly I realized I didn't even know what to call him. "Uh, what's your name?" I asked.

"Doesn't matter," he answered. "You should get out of here if you want to make it back to Midnight proper before dark."

I returned home like a dog with its tail tucked between its legs. Was he right? Was I just being naïve?

Taro appeared in the stables as I brushed down my horse and put away my equipment. I didn't want to talk to him, and he didn't force the issue. He did shadow me back to the main building.

Taro had never asked me to be a slave. He had only asked me to be grateful and polite, just as he was. He had never hurt me. He had given me the best of everything throughout my childhood.

I turned, tears in my eyes, and Taro pulled me wordlessly into his arms.

I don't care, I told myself. *Is it my job to sacrifice myself, my comfort and freedom, because the world is not a good place? My selling myself to the Azteka or the Obsidian guild won't make the evil in this world go away. It won't make Felix live or undo Calysta's death. Why should I hate Midnight and turn against it for giving me the privileged life denied to so many others?*

I tilted my head, exposing my throat—the best apology I knew how to make. I needed to bleed, and my blood was the only gift I had to give.

Taro didn't hesitate.

He was gentler than Jaguar had been, and when he let me go I was barely light-headed. He held my arms a moment, until we were both sure I was solid on my feet, and then said, "See? That's what it's supposed to be like. You still don't want to push yourself too hard, though. I'll walk you to your room."

I nodded. "Thank you."

Near my door we passed Elisabeth carrying several rolls of different-colored cloth. I had been avoiding her since that day in the stables.

She was probably on her way to the tailor, but she didn't reach her destination; she swayed on her feet, and the rolls of cloth went tumbling down to the ground, creating a rainbow on the thick carpet. She scrambled to pick them up but collapsed to her hands and knees instead, retching dryly.

Despite my own light-headedness, I knelt to help her.

"What has he been doing to them?" Taro muttered to himself. Then he stepped forward to ask, "Girl, you're one of Jaguar's, aren't you?"

She looked up and nodded sharply. "Yes, sir."

When Taro reached out to offer her a hand, I saw her

flinch. He waited, and she eventually accepted the offer. However, the moment his skin touched hers, he frowned.

"You're burning up," he said. "How long have you been ill?"

"I did not realize I was, sir," she replied, her gaze downcast.

"Get to the infirmary. Stay out of the kitchens. Leave the fabric. Send someone else to pick it up." He delivered the swift string of commands with enough irritation in his voice to make my skin crawl. In spite of how sick she was, Elisabeth jumped to obey. "This is what happens when bleeders don't take care of themselves," Taro said to me after the woman had darted away. "I'll have to check on everyone in her group to make sure she hasn't spread it. Vance, go get some rest."

He walked away, steps swift and posture tight. I stayed on my knees a few moments longer, trying to calm my racing heart. It was much easier to trust him like a father when he wasn't barking orders and clearly annoyed that a human was ill.

That's what humans do. They're not immortal. They die from sickness, from frailty, from age.

I didn't want Elisabeth to die.

Maybe I could help. I couldn't get sick, so I wouldn't be in any danger if I volunteered in the infirmary. Maybe I could stop Elisabeth from ending up like Felix. First, though, I needed to recover my own strength. Taro hadn't taken as much blood as Jaguar had, but trying to move too fast still made me nauseous.

I ate a light meal and lay down for a few minutes. By the time I made it to the infirmary, Elisabeth had already been released.

"The fever broke on its own after an hour," the healer explained. "We will keep an eye on her for a while, but the illness was mild and seems to have passed."

Sure enough, when I saw Elisabeth the next day, she seemed fine. Having never been sick myself, I didn't know how to judge what it meant to humans. I was glad to realize I had overreacted.

I returned to my simple life in the stables and rarely visited the main building. Horses were complex creatures, responsive to the emotions of those around them, but they weren't manipulative. That made their company much more comfortable than that of the vampires, with all my conflicted thoughts about them.

They knew I would never use my power, but I still had my own room, which was kept magically warmed even on the most bitter winter nights. I enjoyed the work I did when I felt well enough, and the freedom I had. On one of my stronger days, when it had been a while since I had given blood, Jaguar showed me the road from Midnight proper to di'Birgetta lands. He also pointed out the branch that would have taken us to Kendra's manor, where the yuletide ball had taken place while I lay unconscious from the blood dreams, and implied that I could probably go next year.

That evening Jaguar introduced me to Gabriel, the trainer I had briefly seen when Malachi came to Midnight. He shared much of Jaguar's brash nature and bluntness, which explained why the two men seemed friendly with each other, but my first impression of him was colored by the gray cells of the east wing and the way Malachi's whole body had recoiled when Gabriel asked about his sister.

I almost said no when he asked if I would come to him the next time the blood dreams bothered me. Both Taro and Jaguar had spoken of how powerful my blood was, he said, and he would be "honored" if I was willing to share.

Honored. Really? I doubt it. Aloud, I said, "Maybe," which made him laugh.

"I can see why Jaguar thinks you have potential," he observed. "You're as much of a brat as he is." He said it with a conspiratorial grin.

"Tell him no," Jaguar advised once we were alone. "Gabriel doesn't hear that word nearly often enough."

Maybe he was right, but I was curious, so I went. It was a good excuse to see the hawk who had run from Malachi. I wanted to decide for myself whether Alasdair could really be the cold-blooded killer who had murdered his brother. All I saw when I looked at her, though, was beauty, grace, and a slave's calm, meaningless poise.

CHAPTER 17

MY PEACEFUL EXISTENCE was full of cracks, like the copper strips holding together the colored glass in my old home. Perhaps it shouldn't have surprised me that my new life was shattered by the same person who had ruined my last one.

It had been quite a while since I had seen or heard from Malachi, which was why my heart leapt into my throat when he interrupted my morning ride by standing in the middle of the path in front of me. His silver-white hair seemed to sparkle in the sunlight, and his violet eyes were every bit as intense and unsettling as they had ever been.

"Morning, Vance," he greeted me.

I glanced behind me and could almost see Midnight's stables around a bend in the road. It had been a couple of days since I had seen any of the vampires—even Mistress

Jeshickah—but I knew there were shapeshifter guards in the trees nearby.

"I wonder sometimes why you stay so close to this place, considering how much you hate it," I said. I had no desire to get down from the horse or otherwise move any closer, even to be polite.

I started to push past him. I had my own errands to carry out, no matter what Malachi was up to. No human slaves were supposed to go to or from the main building— something about a fever and quarantine—but the blood dreams had returned two days ago, and now the horses were running low on feed. I needed to speak to one of the vampires, whether or not they were busy.

"Some power has been keeping me out of your dreams," Malachi said as I stepped past him.

"Good," I replied. "I don't want you in my dreams."

"What's going on in Midnight? They won't let me in."

"Why *should* they let you in?" I demanded. "I have my own doubts these days, about a lot of things, but even I can tell you're trouble."

He leaned back against a tree, tilting his head up to keep an eye on me. "I hear they've made you into a bleeder."

"What of it? It keeps me alive." Donating blood didn't hurt, and since the first time with Jaguar it had never left me feeling more than dazed for a few minutes. It was simply one more thing to add to the list of reasons that it

180

didn't really make any sense to leave, no matter what Malachi said.

"Keeps you alive?" he echoed. "So they are threatening you now."

"No one has threatened me except for you," I pointed out. "The pochtecatl told me I needed to let blood regularly or my magic would make me ill."

"The pochtecatl . . ." He frowned deeply. "Yaretzi told me she would try to heal you and see if Midnight was willing to let her buy you and bring you back to Azteka land. She wouldn't have told the vampires to bleed you."

"Maybe she just didn't want me to die."

"Your blood is *sacred* to them," he snapped. "Well, all blood is, but yours in particular, because you have the magic. They wouldn't feed it to those creatures." He shut his eyes and took a deep breath. "Not unless they've become as corrupt as the other kingdoms. I can't—" He broke off as a figure appeared between us. I was on my knees on the ground half a heartbeat after recognizing Mistress Jeshickah.

She was not looking at me, though, but staring at Malachi, who had frozen so still he may as well have been made of ice. When he took his next breath, it made his body tremble, as if that simple act were difficult.

"To what do I owe this visit?" he asked from where he was still leaning against the tree.

Mistress Jeshickah responded by striking him so hard that he fell to the path in front of me, eyes wide. The blood on his lip and cheek looked vivid and horrific on his pale features.

"Traitor," Mistress Jeshickah spat.

"I am a traitor to many nations, and occasionally to my own blood," Malachi said, each word careful and distinct, as if it pained him to speak. He had not yet stood, as if he knew better than to do so. "But I have broken none of your laws, and I have permission to be on Midnight's land. So why—"

She interrupted him with a swift kick. I couldn't help whimpering at the sound of something cracking as Malachi's form flipped over twice before falling to the ground again. I might not have liked him, but that didn't mean I wanted to witness this almost casual brutality.

He started to push himself up, and the next kick caught him in the arm, snapping it.

"Mistress." The frightened squeak that escaped me made her turn slowly, but she was clearly furious.

"Meet us in my study," she ordered. "Go by wing. *Now!*"

I cast one last, frightened glance at Malachi and then changed shape and returned to the main building of Midnight as quickly as my underused wings could take me. The guards at the front doors let me in, and another set of guards unlocked Mistress Jeshickah's study when I repeated her commands in a terrified stammer.

She had called Malachi a traitor. Had he planned to hurt me? Was that why she had greeted him that way? Or was it worse, and she thought I was involved in whatever he had done?

I nearly tripped over the body on the floor. I flung myself back as I recognized the witch I had last seen chained in the back cell. His skin was blotted with bruises and cuts, and his neck had been twisted at an unnatural angle.

My eyes kept straying to that battered body as I curled up in an armchair to await my fate. The notion of running or hiding never occurred to me. I had nowhere else to go. Besides, I had run when Lord Daryl had assaulted me, and that had resulted in total disaster.

I would accept whatever happened next.

But I couldn't get the sound of Malachi's bones breaking out of my mind.

When Mistress Jeshickah entered the room, she was holding Malachi by the scruff of his neck. She threw him down to the marble floor not far from the dead witch, and at first he just lay there like a rag doll on the polished cream-and-black marble. Blood was dripping from many places now, and my mind couldn't quite make sense of the direction some of his bones had taken.

One of the healers followed them in. Expressionless,

she set about pulling bones into place and splinting them. Malachi had his eyes and jaw clenched shut, but small whimpers still found their way out in place of the screams he was trying to suppress.

"I know how fast your bones heal," Mistress Jeshickah explained to him in a soft, cooing voice. "I wouldn't want to permanently disfigure you by letting them set all wrong, now, would I? Not yet, anyway." She patted him on the shoulder, hard enough to make one of his screams escape.

Another pair of slaves had just carried in a basin of steaming water. Mistress Jeshickah ignored the rest of us as she diligently washed blood from her hands and arms before passing the soiled towel back to the slaves who had brought it. Suddenly, Jaguar's joke from long ago about Mistress Jeshickah's obsession with her bath no longer seemed funny.

Now clean of blood, she watched impassively as the healer continued her work.

"That should be sufficient, Mistress," the healer said softly, after checking Malachi one last time.

Mistress Jeshickah nodded sharply and then gestured for the healer to leave. "Take the corpse with you," she added. "I have what I need from it. As for you," she said to Malachi. "I will return once your jaw and windpipe have had a chance to heal. Then we will speak. Vance, perhaps you can convince your friend here that further lies will not serve him well."

She left, as did the healer with the witch's body over her shoulder. I heard the click of the lock sliding into place.

"What have you done?" I asked Malachi, in a panic.

He lifted his head laboriously toward me, coughed, and then shuddered at the pain the movement caused. The cough had brought more blood to his lips. He tried to speak and then started coughing again.

I heard the thread of his voice in my mind. *Can't talk yet. Things broken.*

The images were disjointed, not nearly as coherent as his dream voice, but I could mostly make sense of them.

"Can I do anything for you?" I asked. I still believed that he was responsible for whatever Mistress Jeshickah blamed him for, but it was hard to look at him lying there, fighting the pain, and not help.

Tell me. Why?

"You really don't know?" I asked, but I knew he would not necessarily admit anything more to me than he had to Mistress Jeshickah.

Don't know. Don't want to die for something not my fault.

"Neither do I," I answered.

What going on?

"I don't know."

Must know something. What has been happening here? Why is she angry?

I shook my head. I didn't know. I had barely even seen any of the vampires lately.

"They've been keeping the household slaves and stable hands apart to avoid sickness in the stables," I told Malachi, "so I haven't even been in the main building for the last week."

Malachi stared at me as if I had just said one of those things he found incredibly stupid. At least this time I realized why it was stupid.

I rephrased. "There's some kind of illness being passed among the slaves," I said. "No one in the stables has caught it, though, so I don't know anything but rumor."

How many people have it?

"I don't know," I responded.

Malachi pushed himself up a little more and rotated his shoulder slowly, wincing. He cleared his throat and said in a rough voice, "Perks and pitfalls of healing like a falcon."

"What?"

"I told you before, my father was a falcon," he said. "They heal fast. Jeshickah knows it. It's nice not to die easily, but if she thinks I'm involved in some kind of slave plague, I'm not sure I want to heal this well."

"It's not a plague," I protested.

It took him three tries, but he managed to stand. One leg still wasn't working well, but he crossed to the door and put his hands on the wooden paneling.

"Want to come for a walk with me?"

"What?" I yelped. Why did everything he ever said take

me off guard? "No. We're supposed to stay here. She'll be furious. And anyway, it's locked."

He reached down and opened the door. "There aren't many locks that hold me in," he replied. "I'm not going far. I just want to get a sense of what's going on here. Otherwise I won't know anything when Jeshickah comes back, and our lot will not have improved at all. You do want to be able to answer her questions, right?"

When he put it that way . . . "You're manipulating me because you know I want to help her. You don't want to help her."

"I want to survive, which might mean helping her, so our goals are not incompatible," he replied. "And yes, I'm manipulating you. That should be familiar to you, since I'm fairly certain that's almost all that anyone does to you."

"Why do you say things like that?"

And why did I go with him when he stepped forward into the hallway?

It was late morning, which was normally a quiet time, but even so the halls seemed unnaturally still.

"We could ask Jaguar," I suggested. If anyone would answer my questions without being angry, it was Jaguar.

Malachi made a choking noise—maybe his throat wasn't quite healed yet—but followed me. I knocked on the door.

I waited a long time. He might be busy, or sleeping . . . but this was important. We needed answers before Mistress Jeshickah returned. So I knocked again, louder.

As usual, Celeste opened the door.

"Is Jaguar in?" I asked.

She shook her head. At the same time I heard her stomach rumble. Looking closely, I saw that there were dark shadows under her sightless eyes.

"Are you okay?" I asked.

Malachi, behind me, asked, "Are you sick?"

"I'm not sick," she answered.

"She's a quetzal, too," I explained to Malachi. "She can't get sick."

But she can starve, I thought. It was Jaguar's responsibility to take care of her. He had said as much to me. Why wasn't he doing it?

"Do you know how many are ill?" Malachi asked.

We didn't get an answer before a cold voice made me turn. "If you're up and wandering around," Mistress Jeshickah said, "it must be time for us to continue our conversation."

I tried to kneel, but Malachi caught my arm.

"It isn't just the slaves who are sick, is it?" he asked, this time not freezing or flinching in the face of her wrath. "The trainers have it, too."

I was sure she would laugh and call him a fool. After all, he had to be wrong. Vampires didn't get *sick*. They *couldn't*. That was part of what set them apart from humans.

I waited for her to laugh, but she never did.

CHAPTER 18

MISTRESS JESHICKAH NODDED.

"There is no natural illness in this world that affects vampires, so you assume it is magical," Malachi surmised. "You have plenty of witches on your payroll, but you don't want to consult any of them because they might turn on you if they see that you are this weak. Am I correct?"

"As one of the creatures of magic who has been near this place recently, I am sure you understand why I feel we must talk," she replied.

"If I had the power to cause a plague among your kind," he said, "I would have used it when my brother was still alive."

"If you are so clean of guilt, then why are you lingering in our lands?" Mistress Jeshickah asked. "You have no connection to this boy, yet you stay near him and bid to buy him from us. You do not return to the sister you so melodramatically claim to have sold your soul to save, and yet you expect me to believe you have no hand in recent events?"

"Why are you not sick?" Malachi asked, ignoring her questions. "Has it spared any of the others?"

"The disease spread through the stock," Mistress Jeshickah explained. "Once the first fever passes in humans, there is no sign of the illness for quite a while, so many of the infected bleeders returned to the rotation before we realized they were sick or that they would make us sick. I do not feed from the public stock."

"You need a witch," Malachi said. "Even if I were responsible, your beating me bloody wouldn't heal your boys. And since I am *not* responsible in any way, I would appreciate it if you continued to follow your own laws. I'm freeblood. That means you can keep your hands off me as I *leave.*"

"You brought the quetzal back to us," Mistress Jeshickah said as Malachi turned away.

"I am not responsible for the way your property behaves," Malachi replied.

"That would be relevant if Vance were a slave," she snapped, "but as you've been told repeatedly, he is *not.* He is as free as you are, and when *you* assisted his return, he came to us as a plague bearer. That could be taken as an act of aggression every bit as much as if you had walked in here with a hunter's blade."

"This is *my* fault?" I asked.

They both looked at me with an expression that said, "Oh, the child is talking again."

"I made Jaguar sick," I said, putting the pieces together. "Elisabeth was his. He gave it to her. But he got it from me. I didn't mean to! I didn't know—"

"You can't help it if your blood is, apparently, poison," Malachi interrupted. "There are other witches who have the same trait. Perhaps the vampires should have considered that *before* passing you around."

"I've never owned a bloodwitch, but I have had the opportunity to feed on one before," Mistress Jeshickah replied. "This is not typical. I thought at first the assassin-witch might have done it, but when I interrogated him he admitted to sensing the poison in my protective little quetzal when they fought in the stables." Those last words didn't sound as fond as they should have. "I killed him, just in case, but his death had no effect."

"A spell this powerful wouldn't survive the death of the witch who cast it," Malachi murmured in agreement. "As for others . . . Vance, you were in the market just before this all started. Any stranger who bumped into you or said 'excuse me' in the crowd could have been a magic-user. If the spell was prepared ahead of time, it could have been stored in anything, and cast with a simple touch."

"Malachi," Mistress Jeshickah said, "you will discover what has been done to the quetzal and how it can be undone."

"No," Malachi replied. "This is your hole. Dig yourself out, or don't. I'm not involved."

"Let me make myself clear." Mistress Jeshickah stood before Malachi, wearing the perfect, quiet calm I recalled from after the assassination attempt. "You *are* going to fix this. If you fail and any of my men die, or if you run, I will track you down. I will wipe your guild off this map. I will take your precious sister's future mate, make him the first of my new trainers, and then have him break her under his heel. I believe that would fulfill the prophecy of which you are so fond."

It would be hard to believe that Malachi could pale any more, yet I was seeing it. He seemed to become nearly transparent as he nodded silently.

"The lower cells are empty," Mistress Jeshickah said. "That should be a comfortable enough space for you two to work in."

Malachi's gaze rose swiftly, and he protested, "Vance won't survive down there."

"I can't imagine how you intend to work on this problem without studying its origin. If you're concerned for Vance's health, you had best work quickly."

"I doubt you'll let me look at the trainers, but it might help if I examined one of the ill bleeders."

There were words I wanted to say and questions I wanted to ask and screams building up in me, but I could not make a sound as I followed them to the last door in the hall. During my tour Jaguar had said only, *This is . . . also none of your concern, because it will always be locked. This is a working building, Vance.*

Knowing now what "work" the trainers did, I knew what I would see even before we stepped through the doors. We descended steep stairs, then came to a room with rough stone walls and a dirt floor.

If the cold, slick marble room behind Jaguar's room had been bad, this place was infinitely worse. I could *feel* the aura of despair pushing in from all sides.

Or maybe it's just my own.

I missed Mistress Jeshickah leaving. She was simply gone. She hadn't disappeared; my mind had blanked out for a few moments. I was having trouble thinking and following what was going on. Like the loose, crumbling mortar in the walls, my world seemed to be turning to dust and revealing all sorts of sharp edges and hidden evils.

I remembered Malachi saying once that "they" had been very careful with me.

I understood what he had meant now. Even after I had been exposed to the brutality that was apparently commonplace in Midnight, I had been sheltered from the idea that I could ever be the victim. They had worked so hard to convince me that everything I saw was necessary. Inevitable.

Malachi was at the door, examining it, but eventually he admitted, "This is not a lock I can trip. It's warded magically."

"Are you a witch or not?" I asked. "You obviously have magic, but you told Mistress Jeshickah that she needed a witch, as if you weren't one."

"I'm a little bit of a lot of things, but not much of a healer," he said. "And you're stuck here with me, unless we can buy our way out by saving the lives of the trainers."

"Are you going to?" I asked. Given the way he felt about Midnight, he might choose to die first.

"If Jeshickah were sick, I'd kill myself and you before they could try to break us, and hope that with her death Midnight might fall," Malachi said. "I *should* probably refuse to help anyway, out of principle, but you may have noticed that my principles are a little less honorable than that. Losing the trainers will weaken Midnight, but Jeshickah has made it clear that she will simply create more."

"Would she really go after your family?" I asked.

"In a heartbeat. Metaphorically speaking, since she doesn't have one."

"What prophecy is she talking about?" I asked. Visions of the future had been common in Lady Brina's myths, but I hadn't thought they existed in the real world.

"My prophecy," he answered. "One that I have been doing everything in my power to bring to fruition. When I

was a small child, I had a vision of my sister on the serpiente throne, with a king who refused to bow to Midnight
as Midnight burned."

I could understand how the vision could be understood in two ways. A king who refused to bow to the empire might help bring about its downfall. Or, if Mistress
Jeshickah followed through with her threats, a king who
was already one of the leaders of Midnight would not need
to bow to it.

"*Can* you heal them?"

"I have no idea."

No matter what Malachi said, or even what I saw, I
didn't really want the trainers to die—partially because of
Mistress Jeshickah's threats, but also because I didn't think
I could stand it.

I had seen the darkness. There had been moments when
even Jaguar made my skin crawl, or when he looked past
me as if I were so far beneath his notice that I might as
well not have been there. I had seen instants of anger and
irritation quickly subsumed beneath his placid, affable
mask. I had seen Lady Brina's rage and Mistress Jeshickah's
calm viciousness. I had seen the way Elisabeth had flinched
away from Taro in fear. And of course there had been those
"experiments."

But they were my world, my parents and guardians and
teachers. I had been raised to love them, and even if my

mind could now see the evil within and my common sense told me not to trust and not to have hope, my heart wasn't quite ready to let go.

Malachi and I explored the confines of our prison. The door to the outside was heavy wood with a raw finish, lacking a doorknob or latch on this side. The walls were rough gray-black stone, held together with mortar—except for one side, which was solid stone, with iron rings and hooks set into it at intervals.

There was one more doorway, which led to a small and cramped but clean washroom.

"Jeshickah is fanatical about cleanliness," Malachi said as he examined the running-water facilities, which seemed so out of place in a hole like this. "She uses technology humans forgot centuries ago when Rome fell, combined with every scrap of science they discover now. Granted, it keeps her human stock healthy most of the time, but the level of obsession makes me wonder what she experienced as a human."

Jaguar had admitted to me that he had been born human, and that Mistress Jeshickah must also have been, but I still wasn't able to picture her as anything other than the indomitable creation she was now.

I prowled around the main room uselessly. Malachi seemed to be looking for something, and I echoed his movements, but I found nothing but more evidence of horror.

The walls and floor had been splashed and soaked with

dark liquid, probably on numerous occasions. I knelt down and reached out to touch, but then stopped. I did not have to stretch my imagination far to guess that the stains had been left by blood.

"What do we do now?" I asked Malachi.

Malachi took one last look around the cell, sighed, and then sat with his legs crossed. "I'll go into a trance and see if I can trace any patterns of magic connecting you to the trainers," he said.

"And if you can?"

"Then—" He broke off with a choked sound of frustration. "Vance, I have *no idea* how a bloodwitch's magic usually works, or how a poison spell like this might. I don't know if I will find power connecting you to the trainers, or if I could break such a connection if I found it, or if breaking it would even *help*. So I'm going to start small and see what there is to see."

"How?"

"Sit with me."

I sat in front of him, mirroring his position. "What now?"

"Close your eyes."

I did as instructed and felt him take my hands in his, so his thumbs rested over the pulse points in my wrists.

Let your mind wander. You don't need to focus on anything in particular.

How did he talk in my head that way? Did that thought

count as something particular or as wandering? I had no idea what I was supposed to be doing.

Mostly I fidgeted, until Malachi finally took his hands away. I opened my eyes to see him shaking his head.

"Damn it," he whispered. "Your power is too different from mine. I can't make any sense of it, or tell if something isn't working the way it's supposed to. Maybe I'll be able to do more by looking at one of the sick humans. Any magic in them would have to be foreign."

I stood up slowly and discovered that my legs ached from sitting on the hard ground. How long would we be locked in here?

Malachi stood up after me and then put a hand out to catch himself on the wall. Bowing his head, he whispered, "Sorry. It sometimes takes a while to ground myself again."

I walked as far away as I could, trying to give him space, but there wasn't much space to be had. I pressed my hands against the smooth, cold wall and then stepped forward to rest my cheek against it as well. The cold was nice. The air felt too hot. It was stifling.

"Malachi—"

"Give me a minute, Vance."

"Okay."

I paced back and forth. I could only take a couple of steps in each direction. I couldn't even stretch my legs properly. I went into the washroom and put my hands under the water, but it was lukewarm.

Like blood.

I wished I had a towel to dry my hands.

I returned to the cell, where Malachi was kneeling with his body bent forward so his forehead and palms were against the dirt floor. Whatever he had tried to do had obviously taken a lot out of him, and I didn't want to bother him, but I also didn't want to just stand around doing nothing.

I dragged my hands over the rough fieldstones, scraping my palms hard enough that the pain made me shudder. It also helped calm me. I was being silly, a scared little bird. I had to be stronger than this.

CHAPTER 19

WHEN THE DOOR opened I was sitting calmly in the corner, focusing on my breathing and letting my mind go quiet. In my head I wasn't in that cell. I was in the forest. Not the forest I had walked through with Malachi or ridden in with Taro and Jaguar; the trees in my mind were larger, lush and vibrant, with flowers in colors I had never seen even in Brina's paintings.

Mistress Jeshickah's boot heels made dull clunks on the earth floor. Two humans followed behind her. One was a young man who was pale from lack of sunlight but still seemed healthy. His brown hair was clean, and his green eyes were clear . . . and yet they seemed strangely flat when he looked at me. Was that the illness, or something else? Maybe it was related to the semiconscious woman he was carrying. Her hair was matted and hanging in her face, which was flushed with heat even though she was shivering.

"They both have it," Mistress Jeshickah said as Malachi and I lifted our heads, pulling our minds back to our bodies. "The girl is at the height of the fever stage. It will pass within the hour. The boy is near the end of the dormant stage. He will be fine for another few hours, until sunset."

"Is that how long the dormant stage lasts," Malachi asked, "or does the change always happen at sundown?"

"Always at sundown," she replied.

"These two are both completely human to begin with?"

"Yes."

"I might need tools," Malachi said, speaking quickly, as if he was concerned she would leave before he could finish. "Azteka magic depends on bloodletting. A blade could be useful."

Mistress Jeshickah drew a dagger from a sheath at her waist and handed it to him, obviously unafraid that he might turn it on her.

Malachi took it and then leaned back so his head thunked against the dirt. "If you were a little less evil, you might have a *qualified* witch who you trusted do this."

"I tried being kind and trusting," Mistress Jeshickah replied. "My subjects became arrogant and turned on me. It is indeed better to be feared than loved."

She walked out, closing the door and locking us in

again, this time with two sick humans and no more hope than before.

"Bring her here," Malachi said to the slave.

He laid the unconscious woman down in front of Malachi. "She has not been able to stay awake," he said.

"That's fine," Malachi answered. "I work better through dreams, anyway."

He put a hand on her sweaty brow and closed his eyes, his body going impossibly still.

"What's your name?" I asked the other man.

"Joseph."

"I'm Vance."

He nodded, but his eyes never lost that strange emptiness, even when he looked straight at me.

"How many people are sick?" I asked.

"Not many now," he answered. "Eight, if she is the last."

Eight still seemed like a lot. It had only been a couple weeks. "After the dormant stage, how long does it take people to recover?"

"Pardon?"

"There's the fever, and then the disease goes dormant," I said. "Right? And then what happens? You said not many now, so how long does it take people to recover?"

"The fever returns," he answered, with no emotion in his voice. "The throat turns black here," he said, gesturing to the spot on his throat over the pulse, where the vampires would have fed, "and then it spreads out like blood poisoning. At least, in the bleeders it starts in the throat. We think one of the cleaning crew picked it up when scrubbing blood from one of the cells. Her hands blackened first. In one of the healers, it started in her knee, we think from where she knelt in the blood while working on someone down here. In the slave from the stables, it spread from the wounds on his chest. He was first, but we assumed it was a normal infection caused by his wounds."

The slave from the stables. Felix. He was talking about Felix. None of the vampires would have fed on him while he was working in the stables, but I remembered reaching out, drawn by his blood. I had touched it, before coming to my senses.

That was why he had died. *I* was why he had died. That whispering . . . had it actually been my own power, or had it been the contagion, seeking release?

"And after that?" I asked.

"Madness, when it reaches the brain," he answered. "Screaming. We put them out then. Mistress Jeshickah told us to suffocate them, to make sure none of the blood was spilled."

And this is my fault?

"How many so far?"

"I will be number twelve."

"How can you be so calm?" I whispered. "Don't you care?"

He frowned a little before asking, "Why?"

"If we can't cure this, you are going to *die*," I said. "Insane and in agony, by the sound of it. You don't seem afraid. I'm terrified. Please, tell me why you're not."

He shook his head. "I'm sorry. I don't know how to answer that."

Those were the exact words Elisabeth had used when I had asked her what it meant for a slave to prove herself.

Malachi's eyes opened. He drew a deep, ragged breath before saying to me, "Vance, you're talking to a slave in Midnight. Whether he was born here or born free and then broken in these cells, the spark of free will required for one to care about self-preservation has been stripped from him. He doesn't care because he has nothing to care about."

"That's . . ." *Felix. Elisabeth.* Jaguar had been so insistent that they didn't mind.

I had been so willing to *believe* him. If Malachi was right, then in a way Jaguar had been honest. They didn't mind, because they weren't allowed to. They didn't know *how* to.

"That's what trainers *do*," Malachi said with a shiver. "At least it's easier to move around through the dreamscape when there isn't a spark of self-awareness to interfere."

"What did you learn?" I asked hollowly. "Can you cure it?"

"Her fever dreams are the same as the blood dreams I had the misfortune of finding when I searched for you mentally," he answered. "The first fever is probably a side effect of the magic taking hold. The body comes to terms with it for a while, so the illness seems to go dormant, but humans don't naturally have magic. They can't sustain it. I'll examine you next," he said, speaking to Joseph, "but I suspect that the magic in you is almost gone. Give me your arm."

Joseph did so without asking questions. I was the only one who yelped when Malachi used the knife Jeshickah had given him to cut across the back of Joseph's forearm.

The blood that spilled onto the dusty floor was a sickly orange color, with bits of gray-white pus floating in it like dead insects drawn to rotten fruit. I gagged, pushing myself away. Even Joseph, staring at the diseased fluid trickling out of his own body, looked disturbed.

"Magic is the only thing keeping you alive," Malachi said. "Blood magic is also fire magic, so the sun probably sustains it. When the sun sets the last of the magic dies, and your body has to try to function using *that*." He pointed to the growing puddle on the floor.

Joseph continued to stare. He didn't ask any of the questions I would have asked, but neither could he pull his eyes away from the wound.

"Sorry," Malachi said to Joseph. "Let me take a quick look to confirm, and then I'll make you more comfortable."

Why did neither of them bother to put a hand to stanch the flow of that . . . I couldn't think of it as blood. It wasn't blood. It was more like bile, and it kept dripping slowly,

206

clumping and congealing on the dirt as Malachi closed his eyes again to search Joseph's power.

My heart began to beat wildly. It was so *wrong.* This was all wrong.

I couldn't have done this.

I looked from one sick human to the other. My fault. I couldn't have known. The Azteka had told me . . . had Yaretzi told the vampires to feed on me? Not directly, but she had led Jaguar in that direction, while remaining vague enough that he would trust her motivations.

She knew what would happen.

I was sure of it. She knew how this power worked. And she hadn't just known what would happen when she came to "save" me, in that act of mercy that had so confused Malachi. She had known when we first met in the woods. She had established that I wanted to return to Midnight—that I was *loyal* to Midnight—and then she had given me to them. She had only saved my life later to ensure that the plan progressed.

Had Malachi known, too? He had said he would try to rescue me, but maybe that had been a ruse so he could stay close and track all these events. Now he was trying to save his own life, theoretically, but in reality he had yet to say he could do anything to help.

Malachi had said, more than once, that he and others manipulated me—easily and frequently.

Well, I was sick of it.

I didn't want to die because strangers had decided to maneuver me into a position where I would become a plague to everyone around me, humans and vampires alike.

Of course, I didn't have much say in my fate now, did I? I was locked down here in this tomb, with a man who may or may not have been involved in organizing this disaster and two humans who might as well already have been dead.

I leaned my forehead against the cold wall again and tried to bring my mind back to the lush jungle I had found in my head before, but it was so hard to put myself there when all my fears and doubts and despair were right here, locked in with me.

A wet snap made me jump. I twisted about to see Joseph slump with a broken neck.

Malachi set the dead human down gently as I shouted, "What are you *doing*?"

"Making him more comfortable, like I said I would," Malachi replied. "Or would you prefer to wait until he was screaming in pain and madness?"

"How could you . . . you . . ." I understood *what* he had done, but not *how*. How could he, with his bare hands, have broken bone and sinew such that the poor, hollow-eyed human's life ended in a blink? How could he stand it?

How many times had he killed?

"Am I next?" I asked.

"I very much hope not," he answered. "Unfortunately, that decision is probably going to be left to Jeshickah. I can't do anything down here. This doesn't seem to be a complicated spell, but that doesn't mean I can do anything about it. The only thing I can tell is that there isn't any observable connection between the infected humans and the trainers. Whatever poison has passed to them, it is working on its own now. The humans it infected along the way were rats carrying plague, nothing more."

"The pochteca knew this would happen," I said, sharing my suspicions and watching his face to try to determine whether he was involved, too.

Malachi shrugged. "Maybe they did. Mysterious are the ways of the Azteka."

"They must have. That's why she saved my life."

"I considered that," Malachi said, "but if the Azteka knew the blood of one of their witches could cause this kind of destruction in Midnight, they would have made up an excuse to sell one of their own in long ago. They would have sent someone who would be able to manipulate the situation and who would make sure to infect Jeshickah."

"Unless they hesitated to sacrifice one of their own but had no such compunction about sending me in, once they realized I was already under Midnight's thumb."

"Azteka don't shrink from self-sacrifice for the good of the nation," Malachi said, shaking his head.

"Why are you defending them?" I demanded. I remembered the way Yaretzi had treated me when we had first met. I had been grateful at the time, since she had given me back to Taro, but now that I better understood what she thought of Midnight, I saw the scene in a clearer light. "They're the ones who should be in this box."

"And they're the ones who *will* be in this box if we imply to Jeshickah that we think they set this up!" Malachi shouted. "I am not selling someone else in to save my skin."

And what about mine? I wondered. Was I allowed to "sell in" the person who had sent me here with no warning of what I would become, and who had led to our being down here?

"Don't, Vance," Malachi said.

"You have done nothing but ruin my life from the moment I met you," I snapped. "As far as I can see, *you* are the most obvious suspect for this plague. You have magic. Back when you still thought I was dangerous, you could have killed me. Instead, you saved my life and delivered me to Midnight. When I was dying, *you* sent the pochtecatl, who convinced the vampires to feed on me. So why should I trust you, or listen to anything you say?"

"I do have one theory," he said flatly, as if my entire tirade hadn't taken place, "about this fever."

"What?" I asked guardedly.

"There's no magical connection between the humans and the vampires," he said, "but I cannot read your power well enough to know whether there might be a connection between *you* and the vampires. There is a chance that killing you might save them. Would you like me to try?"

The words were said so calmly and coldly that it took me a moment to realize he really had said what I thought I had heard.

Killing you might save them.

A few weeks ago I might have accepted that sacrifice as no more than my duty as a grateful child. My life for all of theirs? Easy trade. In the abstract. In reality—

"I don't want to die," I whispered.

Malachi had suggested it as a possibility, not a certainty. What if I knew for sure? *Knew* that, with my death, I could save everyone—the vampires, the humans who were still sick, *everyone*. What then? Was my single life worth so much?

I wanted to scream, *Yes! It's* my *life!*

I didn't choose this. I didn't deserve to die.

Chapter 20

THE DOOR OPENED, and I had thrown myself at Mistress Jeshickah's feet before I realized that if Malachi told *her* that killing me might save the trainers, she would do so in the blink of an eye. I knew my value to her—it was exactly correlated with my usefulness.

"What have you learned?" she asked.

Malachi explained about the slaves' blood, and why they died at the end. He shared his theory about why the Azteka could not have known this would happen and concluded by saying that there was little else he could do from down here.

I made my decision in silence: I would not volunteer to end my life. I couldn't stop Malachi from speaking and knew I had no hope of defending myself if Mistress Jeshickah decided I needed to die, but I wouldn't sacrifice myself, not for anyone. I wasn't a slave, I didn't need to selflessly put my owners before my own well-being. The Mistress of Midnight wasn't *my* mistress. Not anymore.

"Someone needs to look directly at the trainers," Malachi said. "Preferably someone more competent than I am."

"Did you learn anything about our little bird?" Jeshickah asked.

I braced myself. The only decision left to make was whether I would try to run or try to fight, even though I knew either was useless.

Malachi looked at me for a moment before turning back to Jeshickah to say, "I cannot read his power well enough to tell if there is any lingering connection between him and your vampires. However, I have seen what happens to humans when the magical infection is suddenly gone. If Vance dies, it could kill the trainers."

I wasn't sure I hid my shock very well, so I was grateful that they were looking at each other, not me. That was the exact *opposite* of what he had said to me. Had he been lying to frighten me earlier? Was he trying to protect me now?

I was smart enough not to ask.

Instead, I asked, "What is wrong with the . . . the trainers?" Malachi always called them that, and Jeshickah seemed to accept that as a term for all of them, but my first impulse was still to call them all by name. "I mean, exactly?"

Part of me recognized that the precise symptoms might

tell us more about the illness and therefore help us heal it, but more of me just wanted to know what was happening. It was hard to imagine Taro or Jaguar falling ill.

"Good question," Malachi said. "And I think you knew you would need to answer it eventually."

"All of them are unconscious now," Jeshickah said. "It started with vivid dreams and increased hunger."

"Did anyone remark on how odd the dreams were when they first occurred?" Malachi asked. To me he added, "Vampires don't dream."

"Jaguar assumed—rightly—that they were a side effect of taking Vance's blood. Taro did as well. Sometimes that happens when we feed on someone powerful. It has never led to this."

"What kind of dreams?" I asked. Jeshickah gave me a look that asked, "Does it matter?" so I added, "I want to know whether they are the same as the ones I had."

"Jaguar and Taro both described them as pleasant," Jeshickah answered. "They have very different preferences, so I would be surprised to learn the dreams were identical. Normally I would be able to see for myself, but something about the illness keeps me out."

"Can I see Taro?" I asked. "Please. He has always been good to me. I hate thinking about him ill."

Manipulative or not, Taro was all I had known for so long. I needed to know if I could look at his face once more and still consciously decide to put my life before his.

Malachi made a sickened sound and turned away, leaving me to face Jeshickah on my own.

"I didn't mean to do this," I added, pleading.

"You just want to get out of this box," she replied. "Very well. You may come upstairs. As it turns out, I am inclined to believe that you are as innocent as a Trojan horse."

I wished I could argue with her metaphor, but it was too accurate. None of this had been my intention, but the attack had still come from inside me.

"In exchange for your release, you can carry a message to the marketplace for me," Jeshickah said. "You ride well enough to follow the path, correct?"

I nodded. I had been to the market more than once.

"You're opening him up to assassination, you know," Malachi said.

"Perhaps," she replied without concern. "Come with me, Vance."

She left Malachi locked away and took me to her study. As she sat at her desk and began to draft a letter, my gaze was drawn to the black wooden door, now open to reveal Taro, Jaguar, Gabriel, and another trainer lying on the veined marble floor. Blankets had been placed under them as if to protect them from the cold stone, but they didn't seem to notice. Even Taro's dark skin seemed pale and sallow.

I'm sorry, I thought.

"Jaguar thought you had potential," Jeshickah said. I jumped at her voice, just over my shoulder. "Even once the pochtecatl convinced us that your magic was useless, my Jaguar insisted that, in a few years' time, he could make you into a man who would thrive in our world. He thought you could be one of us."

She held out two cylindrical letter cases. "If he survives," she said, "I suppose the offer will still be open. Return, and you can live as a prince. If he dies, then for his sake I will warn you never to cross my path again."

I swallowed thickly and took the letters from her with trembling hands. Malachi had said that trainers took free souls and made them into slaves, stripping them of free will and passion. What had they been trying to twist *me* into?

A man who would thrive in our world. A man who didn't flinch at the sight of blood and pain but accepted a slave's servitude as necessary and right. A man who could dismiss vicious punishment as appropriate, and who could cut into a girl's arm and draw blood for his own gain.

"Deliver these to the marketplace," Jeshickah said, as if unaware of my reeling horror. "One is to be hung on the message post. The guards can show you where it is. The other should be given to the pochteca directly or left on their stall. It will be dark before you return, so you should stable the horse you ride at the market. You may sleep in the guards' cabin if you wish."

"Should I return in the morning?" I asked when I realized she was done with her instructions.

"As long as you deliver those letters and leave my horse in the market stables, I do not care where you go afterward. As I said, *Jaguar* had a plan for you. I have none."

After everything, how did those words still have the power to cut? Old habits. Sometimes the heart is not quick to believe the mind.

"Go now," Jeshickah snapped. "I have no desire to look at you unless you can be useful."

I turned and fled. I did not know what the letters said, and I didn't dare ask. It didn't matter. Whether the letters contained threats, slander, or pleas for assistance, I was powerless to respond.

As I reached the stables and saddled my horse, I tried to squash a twinge of guilt about leaving Malachi behind. I couldn't quite manage it.

I had meant every word I said. I didn't trust him, didn't like him, didn't think he was innocent . . . but neither was I. If Malachi was responsible for the plague, I wanted him far away from *me*, but he didn't deserve to die the way Jeshickah might kill him.

So I rode, with my thoughts lost somewhere between the clouds and the dust. It was not a short ride to the market, and I did not arrive until about an hour before sunset. The square was tightly packed with people of all kinds. They watched me as I stabled Mistress Jeshickah's horse safely before wading into the press of merchants and customers.

Out of the corner of my eye, I saw my friend the Shantel guard watching me protectively. Though he wasn't obviously following me, every time I looked up I could see him just within my field of vision.

I found the message post without needing any help, but the pochteca had not returned to the market yet. Their absence spared me a messy confrontation but also denied me the opportunity to ask any questions as I tacked the second letter to the outside of their stall.

Having accomplished my mission I flagged down the guard so I could ask him the way to the guards' cabin, so I could sleep before . . .

Before *what?* Where was I going to go? Jeshickah had made it clear that she didn't want me around. There was nothing I could do for Malachi, or for any of the slaves dying in Midnight. Malachi had warned that my coming here could be dangerous, but he didn't seem to realize that I still had nowhere else to go. I didn't even know how to find the Azteka if I wanted to.

Someone pushed past me to look at the notice I had just posted.

He read it and swore before looking up at me and then backing away, never breaking eye contact until he could turn and disappear into the crowd.

I took a step back, keeping my eyes on the quickly

growing crowd. I couldn't make out any individual words over the general din of conversation, but I could recognize the growing hostility. What had I just posted?

"You son of a—"

A woman grabbed my arm, shouting at me, but someone else pulled her back. "Leave him alone. You don't want to get involved."

Some continued shouting. Others turned away, as if they either didn't care or were pretending not to care. None of those who were still looking at me appeared friendly.

Why *should* they be? I had never done anything good for any of them. I had been taught to think only of myself and my "betters."

I changed shape and rose above the crowd. A brisk spring breeze above the tree line threatened to push me off course, but I didn't need to fight it for long. I just needed to land by the stables, where the guard quickly found me.

As I saw it, I had only two options: go back to Midnight, where I could beg Mistress Jeshickah to let me work in exchange for a place to stay, or wait for the pochteca and see if the offer to go with them was still open. Either way I knew I would be stepping into life as a servant—or worse: working for either the woman who had made it clear my life meant nothing to her or the people who might have poisoned me.

The decision would be made in the morning. For now, the sun was setting.

"Travel back down that path," the guard directed me once I explained my situation, "and turn left at the fork. The way is a little narrower than the one you took down here, but you shouldn't have trouble finding it. The cabin isn't far. It has its own stables, so you don't have to leave Mistress Jeshickah's horse here with the riffraff."

"Thank you."

"Vance?" he called as I mounted my horse and prepared to head out. "I don't know what you just posted, but it obviously wasn't something that crowd liked. They will blame you for it. Most of them are too selfish or too cowardly to go after the actual trainers, but you would make a good scapegoat for someone who wants to feel big and powerful by killing a kid who is only doing what he was raised to do."

I considered his words as I started down the path he had indicated.

Most of them are too selfish or too cowardly to go after the actual trainers. Didn't I fall into that same category? Didn't *he*? I *was* selfish. I *was* a coward. Even if we could cure the trainers and Jaguar was willing to take me back as his protégé, I couldn't go back to the life I had lived. I would miss his teasing and his irreverent humor, but I didn't want to become the man he wanted to make me.

Suddenly I heard a wavering yelp from up in the trees, and the next thing I knew I was falling from the horse with the breath knocked out of my lungs.

The horse! I thought frantically. I couldn't damage another one. One of the people who had just attacked me had grabbed the horse's reins before it could bolt.

Someone else caught me as I fell, but not as if they were trying to protect me.

I tried to shapeshift, but my captor shoved me down. Then there were cold chains going around my wrists; the next time I tried to change into my quetzal form, I felt the metal at my spine and let out a shriek, falling back into human form.

They dragged me off the path. I looked up to see a half dozen figures around me, all armed with a combination of staves and blades.

"You shouldn't—"

"I'm not afraid," a woman's voice said before one of her fellows seemed to try to caution her back, away from me.

She walked forward until she was standing above me, staring down with her expression utterly impassive.

Her clothes were simple, leather and cloth in the colors of the winter forest, including sturdy boots and gauntlets tipped with copper bands. She wore several daggers of various sizes across the backs of her knuckles. Her skin was fair despite its tan, but what struck me were her pale, moss-green eyes, and hair the color of snow sparkling in the sunlight.

I had only ever seen that kind of hair once before.

"Malachi's sister," I guessed aloud.

"This is extreme, Misha," someone objected from outside of my slim field of vision. "We have no reason to believe Malachi is even in danger, much less—"

"*I* know," the white-haired serpent, Misha, snapped back. "Believe me or don't. I care not."

She knelt down and looked like she was going to say something—maybe something comforting, like "We won't hurt you"—but instead she produced a cloth, which she placed over my mouth and nose. After my first protest and inhalation, the forest around me began to warp and spin. After the second the trees and sky and everything around me turned black.

CHAPTER 21

THE FIRST WORDS I heard, before I even dared to open my eyes, were "The birdie is awake."

Not until you woke me up, I thought groggily.

I tensed and opened my eyes cautiously, as if my enemies might not be able to see me if I didn't look at them. Instead of the white-haired woman, I saw a girl with cinnamon-brown hair pulled back in a large braid, and wide green eyes. Her face had a kind of soft, rounded quality that made her seem friendlier than her weapons indicated. She couldn't have been much older than I was.

"Hi," she said. "Sorry we had to knock you out, but you are like a little puppy dog to the trainers, and we couldn't be convinced you wouldn't show them the way."

I sat up, inching away. My wrists were no longer bound, but I remembered how easily Malachi had caught me when

I tried to fly. I needed to figure out what these people were before I could form an escape plan.

"We hope you will stay long enough to talk," the green-eyed girl said, "but we haven't kidnapped you. You're free to go when you want to go."

I was so tired of people telling me I was free to go only when they knew perfectly well that I wouldn't. "What about my being able to show people the way here?" I asked. If they had to knock me out to bring me here, why would they let me leave on my own?

"You won't learn the way by leaving," she said. "That's how the magic works. You would only know how to get back if one of us showed you how to get here in the first place. Magic is funny like that."

"Yeah. Funny," I repeated flatly, thinking of the magic I had experienced so far.

"We don't intend to hurt you," she said, "unless you try to hurt us first. Which you won't, right?"

"Right," I said. I had no fighting experience. I was not about to assault this heavily armed group.

"Good. Now that we've established all that, you're Vance, and I'm Kadee," she said. "You met Misha earlier. Over there is Torquil. Most of the others are avoiding you." She waved to a man kneeling in front of the fire pit at the center of the camp we seemed to be in. He waved back briefly before returning his attention to the tinder. "You mentioned Malachi earlier."

"You're his family," I said. Though looking at Kadee and Torquil made it obvious the relationship wasn't one of blood, that didn't mean they couldn't be kin.

"Absolutely," Kadee replied. "And who are you?"

"I'm Vance," I said, confused. She knew that; she had *said* it. She had also referred to me as Jeshickah's "puppy dog," and though I didn't like the description, it made it clear that Kadee knew my relationship with Midnight.

"Yes, obviously," Kadee said. "You were abandoned by the Azteka and raised by the trainers. You lived in Brina's greenhouse for a while before moving to Midnight proper. Malachi told us all that. *But who are you?*"

I stared at her. She had just summarized my life. What else did she want?

"That's what has been done to you, or around you," Kadee said. "I want to know who you are, inside, when you think and feel and speak for yourself."

"I . . ." I trailed off, looking around for some kind of inspiration in the sparse camp. None was forthcoming. "I have no idea what you want from me right now."

"Spoken like one of Midnight's pawns. What do *you* want right now?"

Her green eyes were eerily intense.

"I don't know," I said. *A little space would be nice.*

She stared at me a while longer before saying, "I guess that's the best answer we'll get, for now. But you should think about it occasionally. The answer might surprise you." She sat back, cross-legged and no longer hanging over me, which immediately made me more comfortable. "Now on to the rest of the world. Where is Malachi?"

Didn't these people have a leader? Why was I talking to someone my age? "Where's Farrell Obsidian?" I asked. Jaguar and Malachi had both said that he led this group.

I yelped as strong, pale hands dragged me to my feet and then shoved me hard enough to send me sprawling to the ground. I twisted, preparing to defend myself, and found Malachi's sister staring down at me.

"*You* are not allowed to even speak his *name*," she spat. "Kadee may like philosophizing, but I *know* what you are. Filthy bloodtraitor. Bleeder. *What did you do to my brother?*"

Kadee stood up and spoke to Misha, not quite softly enough to keep me from hearing. "Malachi says he's innocent."

"Malachi may be a prophet," Misha snarled back, "but that doesn't mean he can't be a fool. The *trainers* trust this one. That means we—"

"The trainers are sick," I said loudly, interrupting the madwoman's rant before she could continue her argument against me. "Jeshickah blamed Malachi. She wants him to use his magic to fix it. He says he doesn't know how. He kept asking her to bring in a real witch to help her, but she doesn't trust them."

"With good reason," Kadee replied. "Most witches come from cultures that have fought for independence from

Midnight for . . . I don't even know how long. Centuries, I think. The only witches who work *for* Midnight are mercenaries, as likely to accept payment from Jeshickah's enemies as from Jeshickah herself." She met my gaze meaningfully and added, "That's why Midnight has been trying to raise a witch of its own."

"Malachi says he's freeblood," Misha mused. "If he's not a slave, there's no law saying we can't kill him just to make a point."

"Where's Fa—um, your leader?" I asked again, desperately. I hoped he was less bloodthirsty than Malachi's sister and could rein her in.

"Farrell brought us all together, but he isn't our leader," Kadee answered. "We're children of Obsidian."

"Who's Obsidian?" I asked.

"Not who. What," Kadee replied. "Obsidian is an idea. Children of Obsidian believe in free will, individual power, and community strength that doesn't involve kneeling and calling another creature master or king. Originally it was just white vipers, but Farrell made it a place for anyone who was willing to live by Obsidian's ideals."

"Jaguar said you're outlaws," I said.

"That's because the serpiente are ruled by a *king*," Misha broke in, "and that hypocritical coward of a king bows to Midnight."

"What's the other option?" I asked. Stupidly, probably, but I really didn't *know*. "I understand, you say you've chosen not to follow anyone, but isn't the alternative *chaos*? You're outlaws. Malachi has given me the impression that you're constantly on the verge of being caught by serpiente guards, or freezing, or starving. Why would anyone choose that?"

"Because . . ." Kadee started to speak, then paused, staring into the embers. "Because the body isn't the only thing about us that can starve. I had a chance once to live with servants and tutors and all those things, but it would have meant ignoring things that I *knew* were wrong. It would have killed something in me to do it." She looked up at me once more, this time with sadness in her gaze. "I'm not sure that's a decision you can understand yet."

At the moment it wasn't my decision to make. If the trainers died, I wouldn't be welcome back at Midnight even if I was able to stand walking inside those walls with Jaguar and Taro both corpses beneath the ground. Whether I could stand the placid, vacant eyes of the broken slaves around me was irrelevant, since Jeshickah wouldn't give me a chance.

"Can he help us rescue Malachi or *not*?" Misha demanded, clearly impatient with my questions.

"Don't you want to make sure he *wants* to rescue Malachi before we ask him?" Kadee snapped back. "Or do you want to put yourself back in a trainer's cell, at the word of a boy who we know nothing about?"

Silence like an axe falling. Suddenly I could hear my own pulse in my ears.

"Oh, God, I'm sorry," Kadee whispered. "I didn't mean . . ."

Misha spun on her heel and walked off, shoulders tight.

"I would help you save him if I could," I said to Kadee, "but I don't know how. I can't use my magic. I don't know anything about this plague." Because they deserved to know, and I didn't think Kadee would kill me instantly for saying it, I added, "It isn't just Malachi who's in danger."

I reiterated Jeshickah's threat about what she would do to Misha and the Obsidian guild if one of "her men" died.

"Misha doesn't have a mate," Kadee protested, with the tone of one who was objecting to minutiae because the larger problem was too big. Her whole body shook, a violent shudder, and then she focused on me again. "Yet, anyway. It doesn't matter. She still means *us*. Misha, Malachi . . . me. Farrell. We have to do something."

"You!"

I spun around, expecting to see Misha, but instead I faced another hostile woman. Claw marks across her face scarred her tawny skin, and her eyes flashed sapphire blue in the firelight. She stormed toward me, until Kadee stepped forward and put herself between us.

"Aika, calm down! What is it?"

"Do you have any idea what he's done?"

Her shouts were gathering others, who seemed to form at the edges of the clearing like flickering candle flames, sometimes visible from the corner of my eye, sometimes hidden by the Obsidian guild's magic.

"That notice he posted?" Aika snarled. "It nearly started a riot. Midnight is accusing the Azteka of poisoning several of their slaves. They are demanding blood price for those who have died or become useless."

"God help us," Kadee whispered before I could protest that it wasn't my fault—that I hadn't known what was on that paper! I hardly even understood what Aika was saying now. *It can't be good, though*, I thought as Kadee continued. "Aika, I understand you're afraid, but this is not Vance's fault. He's trying to help us."

I felt utterly useless, but I wasn't going to argue with the one person who seemed to be on my side. "What does blood price mean?" I asked.

"For however many slaves Midnight has lost, it is demanding that the Azteka replace each one with something of equal or greater value," Kadee answered. "If they were broken slaves, or second-generation slaves bred in Midnight, the vampires will demand a higher price for them than just one human in exchange."

"That's . . . sick," I whispered, thinking of Felix or Elisabeth being assigned a price, as if they were pieces of furniture.

"Midnight is asking for one shapeshifter for each lost slave, or one healthy, trained bloodwitch for every ten human deaths," Aika added. "With 'greater recompense demanded if further deaths occur,' whatever that means."

"If the trainers die," I whispered. Mistress Jeshickah didn't want to announce to the world that the trainers were sick, but she wanted the culprits to know the punishment would be severe.

"Midnight wasn't specific about what *kind* of shapeshifter the Azteka needed to give them," Aika said. "They could save a lot of their own skins by handing over anyone else they can catch. The members of an outlaw guild no one cares about would be terribly convenient."

Others had drifted up behind her and were sharing what news they had heard.

"The market is emptying out," one young man said. "No one wants to be around when the pochteca get back. We should probably clear out, too."

"I heard some talk about trying to catch and sell in a bloodwitch on their own," another said.

"What does Midnight think it's going to do with a bloodwitch?" Kadee asked. "They're *scary*. I've seen them start fires by touching bare stone, without even kindling. The trainers could control you because they had you from infancy, Vance. Any adult, trained bloodwitch sold in to Midnight is going to go there fighting. Does Midnight really think they can handle *that*?"

I have to ask how you expect to break someone who can in fact boil your blood with a touch.

The trick is not to let them touch you.

"Yes, they do," I answered, recalling the odd conversation I had overheard between Jaguar and Nathaniel the first time I ever saw them. That had been long before this illness. Had they been talking about controlling me, or already speculating about other ways to get a bloodwitch in their power?

"We should pack up and get out of here," Aika said. "Kadee, send the bird away."

"We can't just *run*," Kadee protested.

"That's what we *do*," someone else replied. "We're not an army. If we fight Midnight, we will lose. If we fight the Azteka, we will lose. All we can do is get out of the way."

Around us I saw the shadows of serpents packing up camp. They didn't know that, this time, running wouldn't help. They didn't realize how bad it was.

Across the camp I saw Misha standing, staring at her fellows as they prepared to flee. She looked up and met my gaze, then started picking her way across the clearing toward me.

I braced myself.

"I won't leave my brother in Midnight," she said as she reached me.

"Neither will I," Kadee said.

"Malachi can take care of himself," Aika said. "He always does. Just watch. He'll show up in the shadows any moment, grinning as if nothing has happened. Getting ourselves killed or sold into slavery won't help him."

"He always takes care of *us*." That argument came from Torquil.

"This is why Farrell didn't want us to come here," Aika objected. "Misha, he knew you can't think clearly when Midnight is involved, and you, Kadee, are too headstrong and optimistic to think rationally about *anything*. I'm going back to the main camp. I hope you'll come with us."

"You know I won't," Misha answered.

Aika shrugged. "You're Obsidian. You'll do what you feel you need to do. Just remember we need you, too."

She turned, shrugged her pack onto her back, and started into the woods. When the bustle of exodus died down, only four of us remained: Misha, Kadee, Torquil, and me. Four lost souls, standing in the forest, needing a miracle.

CHAPTER 22

"TELL US," MISHA commanded.

So I did. I described everything that had happened lately, from the blood dreams to the illness among the slaves, and finally to what I had seen in that cell. I had to fight back bile in my throat as I described the fluid that had poured from the sick slave's wound. Misha paced as I spoke, occasionally gritting her teeth or tightening her hands into fists, but she listened without interrupting or threatening. Once more I explained what Jeshickah intended to do if her trainers died.

"She doesn't know who started the plague," Misha said. "She's blaming the Azteka because they're the most powerful magic-users in the market, and Jeshickah knows that cornering them will force *everyone* to respond. She's threatening us because the Obsidian guild tends to do whatever it needs to do. We're a versatile tool, if she can force us to work for her—which she can, in this case."

"How many are dead so far?" Kadee asked.

"Twelve," I said. "Eight more are sick, though, and will probably die soon."

"And then the trainers," Kadee said. "That's a lot of flesh to repay."

"I didn't know vampires *could* die," Torquil said. "Isn't there a chance they'll recover?"

"Everything can die," Misha said. She walked away from us to poke listlessly at the fire.

"Misha shouldn't be here," Torquil whispered fiercely. "Whatever we do, we *cannot* let her go after Malachi if that means entering Midnight."

"What did they do to her?" I asked.

"I don't know," Torquil answered. "She won't talk about it. When they first gave her back to us, she didn't speak for days . . . just woke up screaming in the middle of the night. Malachi stayed with her day and night, until she finally spoke, and her first words were to send him away. She said she couldn't stand to look at him. Now I'm sure she blames herself for his being captured. It's only been a few months since then, and if we put her back in there, back around the trainers . . . I don't think we can predict what she might do."

"Agreed," Kadee said. "Whatever our plan is, we must keep her far away from Midnight."

"Do any of you have magic?" I asked. "You're talking as if we have options."

"We have options," Torquil answered. "We just haven't figured out what they all are yet."

"Malachi will not want us to turn in the Azteka to buy him out," Kadee said.

"As if we *could*," Torquil replied. "Forgetting that selling Midnight a bloodwitch would mean giving them an unstoppable weapon, and ignoring all the pesky ethical questions, an Azteka magic-user would make a bloody smear out of any of us if we tried. I hate to say it, but unless we want to *become* the next generation of trainers, I think our only choice is to try to save them."

My heart leapt in multiple directions. I had wanted to rescue Malachi, if I could do so without sacrificing myself. I *hadn't* expected this group to suggest rescuing the trainers, even if it did appear to be in their own self-interest.

"That is not going to go over well," Kadee answered softly. "Misha—"

"Misha is standing right here," Misha interrupted, making us all jump. I didn't know when she had come close to us again. How did these people move that way? I always stepped on things that cracked and crunched. Misha moved like mist, soundlessly. "And I can be *very* practical, when I need to be."

"Can't we all?" Kadee asked dryly. "A little *too* practical, I think."

"Unfortunately, practicality won't fix this problem," Torquil said. "We need power we just don't have."

"Malachi kept saying we needed someone more powerful than him," I said. "Did he mean someone specific?" I thought of the spells I had seen around Midnight and in the greenhouse. There were obviously *some* powerful witches on Midnight's side. "I know Jeshickah doesn't want the wrong person to know the trainers are ill, but risking the wrong person knowing *has* to be better than doing nothing, right?"

"I like that idea," Kadee said very softly. "Jeshickah is afraid that if the wrong people know the trainers are in such rough shape, they will turn on her. So . . . let's tell the wrong person," she said, her voice more confident now. "Who do we know? We must have *some* kind of contact. We—"

"No," I interrupted, horrified. One minute we were talking about *saving* the trainers, and the next Kadee was suggesting we actively betray Midnight. Torquil spoke the same word, though with less horror and more resignation.

"Malachi will die in that cell if Jeshickah wants him to," Kadee said. "We can't force her to release him, and we don't have the power to bargain, even if we wanted to damn all our souls even further. So let's—"

"Let's all lose our freeblood status by trying to betray Midnight to a witch who might be every bit as much of a tyrant?" Torquil interrupted.

"Freeblood, freeblood, freeblood," Kadee echoed. "We do everything to keep this 'gift' Midnight claims to give us. If we don't cross them and we pay what they ask and occasionally give up a little flesh or a little soul or a child or a brother, Midnight *graciously* allows us to continue doing so. They call it freeblood, but it's just slavery in an invisible cage. Right, Vance?"

She looked at me, and I flinched.

My cage hadn't been invisible. It had been beautiful, even once I started to see the bars.

"This is too big," Torquil said. "I don't disagree with any specific point you're making, Kadee, but *look* at us. If any one of us had ever had luck with making the right choice or trusting the right person, we wouldn't be here, yet we're talking about deciding the fate of our *world*. The four of us cannot be responsible for making this decision."

I nodded. I was *definitely* the wrong person. I wasn't even sure I wanted the trainers dead. I knew what they did, but that didn't mean I could stand to play an active role in their executions.

Though she looked deflated, Kadee still asked, "If not us, then who? Diente Julian of the serpiente? Or Tuuli Thea Miriam of the avians? King Laurence of the Shantel? They already made their choices. They obey and keep their heads down. Even the Azteka, who actually have the power to *fight*, choose to avoid the conflict."

"Fate is like the wind," Misha said. She was standing

right next to me, but her voice seemed distant. "We can face it or we can ride it. In this case fate has handed us four dying trainers and a little bird whose blood is poison. What kind of fools would we have to be to fight that kind of wind?"

"We should ask Farrell's opinion," Torquil suggested. "He might—"

"Farrell is two weeks away," Misha interrupted. "By the time we spoke to him, much less made it back here, the trainers would either be dead or have recovered, and Malachi would be in whatever state Jeshickah felt was appropriate."

"But . . ." Torquil trailed off, pierced by her glare.

"What about you, little bird?" Misha asked me. Her voice had a tone to it that was both familiar and unsettling, but which I could not immediately place. "You could run back to Jeshickah to report us, or you could just run and hide, or you could help. What kind of man are you?"

"I'm fourteen!" I objected, rising to my feet to move away from her. I looked to Kadee, who hadn't seemed much older than I was. We were a bunch of kids, talking about destroying an empire of immortals. "Like Torquil said, this is too big for us."

"It is not too big for me," Misha said. "Would you like to know why?"

"Why?" I asked. How could anyone make this kind of decision?

"After Diente Julian sold us to Midnight," Misha said, "my little brother, Shkei, and I belonged first to Taro and later to Gabriel. I will not say out loud the things that were done to me in the months before Malachi was able to purchase my freedom, only that I am grateful the trainers never really had time to make me into a primary 'project.' Taro was very occupied with you, actually, which is why he kept me a few months and then gave me to someone with more time on his hands. Trust me when I say it was the kind of experience that makes one very . . . well, practical, as I've said. A lot of the little fears and doubts wash away with the blood.

"I have seen the heart of evil. It is called Midnight. If I can destroy it, I will. The world really is that simple."

I looked at Kadee, who was looking at Misha. When the young serpiente's eyes returned to me, I saw fear in them, coupled with knowledge. The trainers might not have broken Misha as a slave, but something inside her was broken all the same.

Her fury still burned bright.

I shuddered. "It can't be . . ." My protest trailed off. I wanted my innocence back, but it was too late. I couldn't form an argument for why Midnight should stand, because now that I had seen its dark core, I knew that all the beauty in the world wasn't enough to justify it.

Jeshickah and the others had raised me the way they did not because they loved me but because it would allow them to control me. Midnight hadn't wanted me. It had wanted my magic.

I loved them, but I could not let them continue.

You have never been asked to die for something, or someone, Malachi had said.

Was this what freedom tasted like?

"What do you want me to do?" I asked, my voice barely a whisper.

"I don't know what you can do, on your own," Kadee answered. "We obviously can't just *let* the trainers die. If we want to try to save Malachi, we need someone with the power to take the heart from the empire, swiftly. Do we know a witch who might be on our side?"

"We could ask the Shantel," Torquil suggested. "They would probably help, if they could."

Kadee scoffed. "A Shantel witch doesn't sneeze without meditating on the matter for a month and then consulting the king," she grumbled. "Even if we could find one, we would need to wait for a royal audience before they would even *listen* to our proposal. Malachi will be dead and the plague will have run its course long before they decide to act."

"There's a Shantel guard in the marketplace," I said.

"He's loyal to Midnight," Misha replied.

"I don't think he really is." I remembered my conversations with the guard, about how he followed Midnight only because he didn't see another option.

"Do you honestly expect us to put any faith in *your* opinion of who we should trust?" Misha snapped.

No one spoke up to argue with her, though Kadee cast me an apologetic glance. Any suggestion I made, I suspected, would be met with the same response.

No other choice, then, I thought. I couldn't justify it to my companions here in the Obsidian guild, but I couldn't get the idea of the Shantel guard out of my head. The increasingly frustrated conversation around me seemed to dim, and his face rose in my mind instead.

Without waiting to ask or hear if they would actually let me leave, I shifted shape. I pumped my wings harder when I saw Misha snatch at my fleeing form and made it above the tree line without further interference.

We weren't far from the road; I was able to find paths I recognized and made it to the market in a short time, even on foot. It was late now, and the only movement in the market was merchants making last-minute deals and packing their wares into wagons so they could flee before the Azteka returned. The Shantel I needed wasn't present, but the other guards were able to give me directions to his home.

It didn't take me long to locate his one-room cabin. I knocked on the door, trembling at the enormity of what I was doing.

Who was I to make this choice? What if Kadee, Torquil, and Misha were at that moment coming up with another option? Surely they knew more about the world than I did.

The guard came to the door, his steps heavy with sleep as if I had woken him. His eyes widened when he saw me, and he asked, "Do you need me?"

Desperately, I thought. *I'm out of other choices.*

CHAPTER 23

"CAN I TALK to you for a minute?" I asked.

"Sure," the Shantel guard answered, giving me an odd look. "Should I put on a pot of tea?"

He didn't wait for me to respond before turning from the door and setting a kettle over the fire.

Though it was about the same size as my "home" in Brina's greenhouse—about the same size as some of the sheds off Midnight's stables—this tiny cabin had a very lived-in feeling, from the tidy bed in the back to the chest and woodstove nearer to the front. There was a knife on the one-person table, sitting next to an unfinished carving; I couldn't tell what the piece of wood would someday be, except that it was obviously intended to be decorative, not practical.

The room was cold despite the hearth. My breath

fogged in front of my face. Even so, the one-room domain had a distinct advantage that my more luxurious cabin had lacked: the real world was outside the door. That made it much bigger, all things considered.

"This is nice," I said. I meant it.

"Thank you," he answered. "But I doubt you wanted to talk to me about how to set up house."

I wasn't sure how to start. I knew he didn't work for Midnight out of loyalty to the vampires, but that didn't necessarily mean he would be willing to stand up against them. His life was comfortable enough. He might not want to jeopardize that.

"How did you end up working for Midnight?" I asked.

He sank into the chair in front of his whittling project with a sigh. There wasn't a second chair, and I wouldn't have felt comfortable sitting on the bed, so I stayed standing.

"You don't know me, Vance," he replied softly. "You don't even know my *name*." Before I could rectify that problem, he shook his head. "Don't bother. I work for Midnight because I once believed I could make a difference here. When I lived among my own people, I spent my time in the *sakkri*'s temple, and shared the visions, and chose my path . . . or they chose my path, or she did. I don't know. But I left because I was told to leave, and then I was told I was never allowed to return. The Shantel do not accept traitors back."

"What is the temple?"

"At any point in life, if one of us feels lost or uncertain, we can choose to dedicate ourselves to the temple for a time—a day, a month, a year, or more. It is supposed to provide guidance. Some stay to study magic. Others learn a new trade or find their mate. It made me restless. I felt as if I had seen the world for the first time, and it was larger than I had ever imagined. I sought stillness by studying with the deathwitch, who prepares the dead for burial, but eventually the *sakkri* told me that the visions I had seen in the temple had left me unfit to remain on Shantel land."

"So you didn't have a choice but to work for Midnight?"

"I work for Midnight because I still feel like I can do . . . something good, somehow," he answered. "We can't kill the vampires. They're too strong. We can hate them all we like, but if we make them into enemies, they will destroy us completely. Our only choice is to work with them so we can make ourselves strong enough to survive."

The question then was: If I told him what was going on, what would he do? He said he had studied for a time as a witch, so he would at least know what Shantel magic was capable of. Would he want to try to help the trainers—or would he support the Obsidian guild's plan and turn on Midnight? Would he report immediately to Jeshickah?

Since he was already loyal to Midnight, Jeshickah would probably trust him.

That was assuming he wasn't too bitter about being

told to leave by the Shantel. He didn't seem to like Midnight, but that didn't mean he wanted to overthrow it.

"What if someone could fight Midnight?" I asked.

My host shrugged. "I don't know," he admitted. "Midnight has spent the last century playing the shapeshifter nations against each other. Sometimes I think that having a common enemy in the vampires is all that keeps most of us from outright war with each other."

That was bleak. What was the point of fighting Midnight if it might only lead to more devastation?

"It's up to you, Vance," he said.

I looked up, confused, because I hadn't said anything.

"The vision I had in the Shantel temple involved me working on one of the vampires," he said. "There was some kind of sickness. Given your anxiety at the moment and the severity of Jeshickah's reaction, I have to assume the sickness in that vision is the one afflicting Midnight now, and that at least some of the vampires have contracted it. You're trying to decide whether or not to ask me for my help. Am I right?"

I nodded slowly. "You're a healer?"

He shook his head. "I am, or was, a deathwitch. My power is with the dead."

"The trainers aren't dead."

He gave me a look that was half pity and half patience. "Vance . . . all the vampires are dead. That is their nature. Magic and power animate them, but their bodies are dead.

I cannot manipulate their minds in any way, but I could manipulate their flesh and perhaps undo damage done by a foreign magic."

"Are you sure?"

"Not sure, no, but there is a chance."

"Are you going to?" I asked. "Now that you know, are you going to go to Mistress Jeshickah and—"

"I already told you," he said, interrupting, "that it is up to you. In the vision I seemed to be helping the vampires, but I could have been concealing my true purpose. The possibility that I would help them with our sacred magic disturbed me so deeply that I had to leave my home, but at that time I did not know all I do now. I only know my power led me to you, just as it surely drew you to me tonight. I will abide by your decision."

"If the trainers die and Mistress Jeshickah does not, she has said she will just start over," I said, "with the Obsidian guild."

My voice sounded far away. I could barely hear it past the pounding of my own heart.

"Children of Obsidian are not easily broken," my host said. "If the Mistress of Midnight insists on starting with them, it may buy us time and win her nothing."

"Time for what?"

He stopped to think but finally admitted, "Time for another miracle, perhaps. The trainers are not the only vampires in Midnight. Jeshickah created them like she created the empire itself. She might be weakened without them, but she will recover."

"Then we need to make sure she's infected, too." Had I spoken those words aloud? Or were they just in my head?

One of the slaves had been infected trying to clean up spilled blood. It did not take much to transmit the disease. If the Shantel witch was in close contact with Jeshickah, and the infected trainers, and me, there would surely be some chance to pass the disease on to . . .

. . . to the woman who had raised me and given me everything.

. . . to the woman who had savagely beaten Malachi and made it clear she had no regard for my life when her trainers were threatened.

"Jeshickah will kill us if she thinks we have betrayed her," I added.

"She will do worse," he replied. "Death is not so bad." He paused before adding, "They say a quetzal can't be broken—that your power will drive you mad and kill you before it will allow you to live in a cage. Is it true?"

"I don't know."

"Maybe we'll see."

With that ominous statement he started assembling the necessary traveling supplies on the bed. "We should leave immediately—if you're sure?"

"I'm not sure," I said, "but I don't think I can stand to

do nothing, either. Besides, your visions brought you here. Who am I to defy fate?"

He laughed as he pulled the drawstring on the bag he had hastily packed. "There is no defying fate. There is no submitting to fate. I do not know if we have free will, only that we cannot know what fate has planned, so we need to *act* as if we make all of our own decisions. This is your choice, Vance. What do you want me to do—try to save them, or try to end them?"

"This is my choice," I echoed. How could this be my choice?

Yet it was, and I had decided.

"If we can end Midnight," I answered, "we should."

End. A gentle word for murder.

Traitor, my mind whispered to me.

Yes, I was. I had betrayed the Azteka and all the shapeshifters by loving the trainers to begin with, and by having a heart loyal to Midnight. Now I was betraying my heart at the whims of my . . . what? My mind, or my soul? Either way I was twice a traitor.

"Why won't you tell me your name?" I asked as we mounted our horses and started up the path.

"My people believe that names have a great deal of power. In this case my concern is that names get put into songs and stories," he answered. "Whether we succeed or fail, I do not think I want to be remembered for this."

Despite the late hour, the road was busy with guards and merchants moving to and from the market, which put an end to conspiratorial conversations. I should not have been surprised when we passed a bend in the road and saw Kadee standing there.

"Torquil convinced Misha to look for the Azteka," she said. "Who's your friend?"

"A Shantel witch," I answered. I started to add more, but another merchant passed us, close enough to overhear our words. "He . . . thinks he can help us with our problem." Kadee would think the witch meant to heal the trainers, not kill them, but I couldn't think of any safe way to tell her the true plan.

"That's convenient," Kadee remarked, casting a baleful eye at the witch. Without asking, she reached toward me and swung up on the saddle behind me.

"It is not convenient when the magic itself tells you where to be," the witch replied.

"Prophecy," Kadee said, shaking her head. "So, you can heal them?"

The Shantel shrugged. "I have never seen a vampire fall ill or even have a lingering injury, so I have never tested whether my magic could possibly heal one."

"At least we can save Malachi," Kadee said, "if we save the trainers."

I wanted to comfort her and tell her what we also intended to do, but it was hard for me to speak, even if I dared

254

risk being overheard. The closer we came to Midnight, the tighter my throat grew and the louder my heart pounded.

The main building of Midnight was surrounded by a high, ominous iron fence. The gates were guarded, but the men recognized the Shantel traveling with me and let us in as easily as the vampires themselves had let my poison into their blood. I wanted to warn Kadee to flee before the Shantel witch gave her permission to enter with us, but couldn't do so without betraying our true purpose.

All my fault.

"Breathe, Vance," Kadee whispered to me, squeezing my hand after I dismounted. "We just need to get through this so we can get her to release Malachi."

My gaze lingered for a minute on the door to the stable loft where I had so recently lived. It hadn't been as beautiful as Brina's greenhouse, but it had been a home. It looked small from here. Maybe I had only just recognized that it could not shelter me when all this was done.

We approached the main gates. Again the guards let us pass, as did the ones on the west wing. Finally we stood at Jeshickah's door.

For long moments we stood there, none of us brave enough to knock. What would we find beyond?

We were still staring when the door opened. Jeshickah stood there, dressed in slacks and a man's button-down shirt that was tied at the waist. Her face was pale, but her black eyes were hard as jet as she regarded the three of us.

"What is this?" she asked.

"We brought a witch," I said. I flinched as the focus of her attention turned to me. For the first time, it occurred to me that she might be furious that we had defied her, even if she believed that we came with help. "I know you did not want one, but when he mentioned his power, I had to ask. I could not stand to do nothing."

Slowly, she looked at the guard.

The Shantel took a half step back. "Pardon our presumption, Mistress," he said, "but I may be able to help. I was trained as a witch before I came to work in Midnight."

She stared again at all of us, each movement lethargic. I wondered whether she had avoided feeding to protect herself from this plague, or whether she was simply exhausted. At that moment she seemed almost pitiable. Almost like a person, instead of the almighty evil power she was supposed to be.

"Very well," she said at last. "You may enter."

CHAPTER 24

THE GUARD GLANCED at Jeshickah for permission before approaching the unconscious trainers in the back cell. There was no expression on her face anymore. She did not look angry, or hopeful, or sad. She just looked . . . blank. Was it exhaustion that had stripped her of all emotions, or was this what she was like when she did not bother to hide her true face?

She gestured for us to go before her, but it took all my willpower to walk through that heavy black door.

The Shantel witch knelt next to a fair-skinned, blond vampire whose name I did not know. Maybe I should have been grateful that the deathwitch had started with someone I had no attachment to, but it felt like he was stalling so I would have more time to panic.

"What will you do?" I asked.

Was he just going to pretend to help while letting them die, or was he actually going to try to find a way to *kill* them? Would it be quick or slow? How long would it take for Jeshickah to realize what we were doing?

"I need to examine them first," he said, "but I think the Azteka magic may have disconnected them from their original source of power. Mistress Jeshickah, if I am right, I may need your blood in order to restore them."

She nodded slowly and then turned away, announcing, "I will be in the study if you require me."

Could she not stand to see them this way, either?

We all watched her leave. In her absence a hush fell.

Jeshickah was so close, only in the next room. She might be able to hear anything we said, which meant I still couldn't tell Kadee our plan or ask the questions I wanted to ask.

I said only, "Can I help in any way?"

"In a minute," the witch answered. "Let me do this."

He turned from us and back to the vampires, putting a hand on the blond vampire's chest and closing his eyes. His expression was deeply thoughtful. His head tilted as if he were listening.

Something inside me broke. I went to sit next to Taro and Jaguar. I put a hand on Taro's and discovered that his skin was clammy. He had raised me in a beautiful cage, and I still wasn't sure if I should thank him or curse him for that. There had always been a world outside that cage—a vast world, which I had only just started to understand and wanted to explore—but it was also harsh and cold and cruel.

As cruel as what we were doing now.

The deathwitch opened his eyes and drew an odd dagger from his belt. Instead of metal, the entire knife—including the blade—was made of wood.

"It's a tool for my kind of magic," he explained when I looked at it quizzically. He gestured for me to come closer. Taking my hand in his, he stretched out my arm as he continued to lie about what he was doing. "I'm bleeding them so I can link my magic to theirs."

He touched the knife to my skin and then paused, looking me in the eyes as if asking permission. I nodded; I could guess what his plan was. I bit my lip to make sure I would not cry out as he pulled the blade across my forearm and then turned it to coat both sides of the wood.

Kadee's eyes went wide as she watched us, her expression unbelieving.

Still holding the knife in one hand, the witch put a palm over the wound on my arm. My eyes watered as searing pain shot up and down from that spot, but I managed not to make a sound. When he moved his hand at last, all evidence of the wound was gone.

When he held up the knife again, the blood had disappeared, as well.

"The blade doesn't hold blood," the witch said, "but

it holds power. I can use it to make a link. Vance, please take this to Mistress Jeshickah. I can link with her power if she lets the blade taste her blood. The wound should be as deep as is possible without damaging her. If what I've heard is true and her kind can survive even a knife through the heart, then heart's blood would be best. She will know how much she can heal."

He held the knife out to me.

Why couldn't *he* do it? Or send Kadee to do it?

I knew the blade was poisoned. I had just watched him link the magic—the disease—in my blood to it. Now he wanted me to take that disease to Jeshickah.

Traitor. Traitor. Traitor.

Yes, I was.

I found Jeshickah where she had said she would be, in her study.

"I heard," she said as I walked in.

She held out one fair hand for the knife.

My body moved, handing the weapon to her without hesitation. I didn't want to give her any more reason to be suspicious. Surely she could hear my pounding heart, smell my anxious sweat.

She must have attributed my distress to concern about the trainers. She wasn't suspicious because she knew I loved them and didn't realize that I had decided to kill what I loved.

She flipped the blade around in her fingers and touched

the tip to her chest, lining the poisoned dagger up with her heart. Could she really survive that?

For the first time I wondered if Lady Brina had been infected, as well. Was she lying somewhere on the floor, perhaps next to a palette of drying paints, wondering why no one had come for her?

My heart choked me.

I didn't say a word.

Jeshickah made a hissing sound as she drove the blade into her body. Her back arched, her eyes shut, and her jaw clenched, but she did not hesitate.

She trusted me.

This woman who was hated by so many, whom I had just killed—though she did not know it yet—trusted me enough to take a knife and pierce her own heart.

An interminable amount of time went by before she let out a breath and slowly, carefully withdrew the blade. It clattered to the floor as she slumped forward, body trembling.

"Mistress," I said instinctively.

"Go," she commanded. "I will recover. Take the blade back to the witch so he can heal my men."

I leaned down to pick up the knife . . . the cursed, poisoned knife.

It wouldn't be long before she realized what had happened. Jeshickah had said that vivid dreams were the first sign of infection, and they would occur as soon as she slept.

Unless she let us go first, she would ensure that we would die with her.

For now I took the knife back to the deathwitch. Jeshickah followed closely. How long would we need to keep up this act?

Long enough, I thought as the deathwitch used the bloodied blade on the trainers. The work looked intricate as he cut a symbol into each trainer's palm. I wondered if it meant anything.

"I can heal you, too," the witch said to me when he was done.

"Heal what?"

"You're carrying death around like a parasite," he said. "It isn't natural."

"You can undo it?" Kadee asked.

The Shantel nodded, then looked up past me to add, "With your permission, Mistress."

"What about my men?" Jeshickah asked.

"They will rest a while longer as their systems destroy the last of the curse," the Shantel witch lied. "They may be weak for some days after they wake, and they will probably need to feed often in order to recover, but time should restore them."

"And the humans?" I asked. "Some of the slaves are still sick. Can you heal them?"

"I can try," the witch answered, "but if the infection is too advanced, there is probably nothing I can do."

Kadee was less concerned with trainers and slaves. "Mistress," she said quietly and deferentially, "would it be possible for us to see Malachi now?"

"Of course," Jeshickah replied. "You might as well all wait with him, until I see for myself that my men are recovering."

I resisted the urge to look at the others, too nervous about what my expression might give away. On our way back to the cells where I had left Malachi, it occurred to me that I could run. *Should* run. All I needed was the tiniest bit of a head start. If I could get outside . . .

No.

Kadee wasn't running. Neither was the Shantel witch. And Malachi couldn't run from where he was.

Kadee reached for my hand and squeezed it as Jeshickah unlocked the door to the cells. Then the sick stench of decay from the two corpses we had left behind rose up to greet us.

Two . . . or three?

Malachi sat against the far wall, his face down on his bent knees. He wasn't moving. Was he breathing? The sound of the door shutting behind us with a thud barely registered in my thoughts as I hurried to his side.

"He isn't dead," the Shantel witch said as Kadee and I both knelt beside the half falcon.

"Malachi?" Kadee called, touching his cheek.

No response.

"What's wrong with him?" I asked.

Kadee shook her head. "He gets this way sometimes. I've heard it was worse when he was younger. It's the falcon magic in him that causes it, I think."

"Jeshickah thought breeding a white viper with a falcon would stabilize the magic without diluting it too much, since white vipers are supposed to have power, too," the witch explained as he knelt beside one of the two dead slaves. Joseph. "Instead she ended up with a child who barely learned to speak, prone to fits of—well, *this*—without any noteworthy power. She would have put him down if Farrell hadn't offered to buy him and his mother."

I looked at Malachi, curled on the floor. He had shown me the place where he had spent his childhood, but I had dismissed his warnings. Because the children weren't freezing, I had excused the lack of warmth in their lives. Because they had food, I had ignored the other ways, as Kadee had put it, that a person could starve.

"What are you doing?" Kadee asked. The witch had turned from us again and was reaching down to close Joseph's eyes.

He ignored the question and, instead of answering, whispered words that lilted musically, which I seemed to *feel* rather than *hear* as they struck me. Like sunlight, or a warm breeze.

As the power faded the witch looked up. "I was trained as a deathwitch. Did you think that meant I just learned how to murder vampires? The dead cry to me. These two, they lost themselves long ago, but their savaged souls still reach out to me. They want to be heard and remembered."

He went to the other dead slave and repeated the process. This time the aroma of baked apples arose, along with the feeling of soft wool pulled across my skin.

"Is there anything you can do to get us out of here?" I asked. I didn't want to face Jeshickah's wrath when she realized what we had done.

"I can do many things," he answered. "For example, I have successfully infected the Mistress of Midnight with a plague. I bound enough of your magic into that knife that a scratch would have been enough, but we convinced her to drive the spell directly into her own heart. Come dawn she will sleep, and she will never wake."

"Then she won't ever know we betrayed her," Kadee said, half hopeful, half skeptical.

"Unfortunately," the witch answered, "there is still nothing I can do to get us out of this cell. I've seen my death here. Maybe another of her kind will do it after she is gone, or maybe we will starve. A locked door can kill us as surely as Jeshickah herself." His eyes flicked to me, and he added, "Sorry. You didn't do anything to deserve this."

"Apparently I did," Kadee mumbled.

"I don't know your story," the witch said, "but you're Obsidian. Whether you chose to join or were forced into it, when you took that name, you traded any hope for a long and comfortable life for what you call freedom. Congratulations," he added. "You're free."

"Jerk," Kadee snapped.

"If it helps, you did change the world, hopefully for the better."

"No," Kadee answered. "It really doesn't—"

The door burst open and we all turned, expecting Mistress Jeshickah. Expecting the end.

The woman who stormed in had the dark, angled features I associated with the Azteka, but I had not seen her before. Her upper arms bore the scars of many small cuts, placed in ritualistic fashion, and her hands held a short bow with an arrow already nocked as she shouldered open the cell door.

CHAPTER 25

THE ARROW FLEW before any of us could move. It hissed by my cheek, the slight breeze of its passing inexplicably hot on my face.

The Shantel witch tried to dodge, but the archer was too close.

The arrow tore into the meat of his upper arm. For an instant time seemed to pause as the witch looked up at the Azteka woman in shock. Then his body jerked. Where the arrowhead had pierced his flesh, the skin sizzled.

He fell to his knees, his other hand moving toward the exposed shaft, as the magic traveled inward. Blood vessels glowed white-hot. For a moment it was beautiful, like moonlight shining in lines beneath his skin, but as that light reached his torso he let out a shriek like nothing I had ever heard.

The sound cut off, strangled, as the witch hit the ground. A cool draft flowed around and through me, drawing a shiver from my bones even before it occurred to me that we had all just been caught. It was over now.

"Alejandra." Mistress Jeshickah's cool, cutting voice floated toward us from the hall. "You seem to have made a mess of my witch."

The Azteka woman set the bow down and held her hands out to her sides. Only then did she turn slowly and say, "We did not commit this crime, and we will not be blamed."

Jeshickah looked at the dead witch and then at the Azteka intruder. "You decided slaughtering my employees would be a good defense?"

"If you attempt to imprison me for his death, you will find it difficult," Alejandra said. "The likelihood of your being able to control me without killing me is low, the likelihood of my killing you in the process is high, and even if you did manage to enslave me, you know my story. I cannot pass on my magic. So you would benefit from hearing me out."

Though she spoke quickly, her words were obviously carefully planned. Despite being in the heart of Midnight and having just killed a man, she was perfectly calm as Jeshickah weighed her words and then said, "Proceed."

"When Yaretzi came to you to take care of Ehecatl, she did so because he was freeblood." It took me a moment to remember that was my other name. "Given the innocence of his upbringing, she did not think it appropriate to let him die for his association with you. We do not kill our children for their childhood misdeeds. Ehecatl," she said, glancing toward me without ever fully turning her back to Mistress Jeshickah, "you are still welcome to return to us, if you choose. I will take responsibility for you and ensure that you are granted every privilege your birth should afford you."

She did not wait for me to answer before continuing to speak to Mistress Jeshickah.

"Our healer *did* notice foreign magic in him, but she did not know its origin. When she explained why Ehecatl would never be able to use his magic, the trainer—Jaguar— concluded that the blood dreams and weakness were results. She did not correct that mistaken assumption, but neither did she lie to any of your people, or encourage them to feed on Ehecatl, or do anything that puts us at fault. She described the poison she sensed in his blood to me when we passed on the road, before I arrived at the market and saw your missive.

"I have told you already, we do not harm children. We would not send an infant or a child to you as a weapon. And we will not be blamed and destroyed because one of *your* traitors from the Shantel felt it was appropriate to do otherwise."

"How could he have—" I started to protest, and then

broke off. I had spoken to this guard for the first time in the market. He had given me his cloak and stayed with me until Taro arrived. "He said . . ." I trailed off. He had said the visions had set him on this path and put him in my way, which was why I had not questioned how easily I found him when we needed a witch. Now I realized it had been even less of a coincidence.

Ignoring me, Jeshickah asked, "What of my men?"

"Now that the deathwitch is dead, his power will fade. Unfortunately, they should recover swiftly."

"Do you require payment for your service?"

Alejandra flinched. "This was not a *service*," she spat in reply. "If he had managed to infect you, I would have volunteered as his protector until your corpse was rotting in the ground. His incompetence is the only reason I interfered. I wish for only one boon in return for this dirty work, one that might even aid you."

I dared not look at Kadee as the Azteka woman spoke her request softly, probably intentionally keeping it from our ears. Alejandra had not known, could not have known, that our nameless Shantel associate *had* managed to infect Jeshickah only minutes ago.

Now he was dead on the floor, and Alejandra had made it clear that with his death, the illness would end.

"May I ask what will happen to us?" Kadee asked. "We did not mean to bring a traitor here."

"Accompany me as I check on my men," Mistress

Jeshickah ordered. "After I see to them, I will decide what should be done with you and your mongrel friend."

We made a strange procession down the halls. Out of the corner of my eye, I saw the few slaves we passed sink to their knees, trembling at Jeshickah's passing. I tried to sear the image in my mind. That was what I needed to recall when I thought of this place.

We all reached Jeshickah's room. Alejandra lingered in the parlor, but I continued forward as if hypnotized. Kadee stayed a pace behind me but did not leave me alone. We held our breath as Jeshickah knelt beside her men.

Jaguar stirred first, his black eyes flickering open for a moment before drifting shut again. I watched tension drain from Jeshickah's body.

"Your clan is not loyal to me," she said to Kadee as the others began to gently rouse, as if from a deep sleep, "but you are more useful outside these walls. Take the mutt from the cells and go. Vance . . ." My heart stopped as she paused to consider. "Jaguar lives, so the offer for you to stay remains open. I look forward to seeing what he might make of you."

My heart gave a little conflicted thump at that comment—a combination of terror and pride. Would I feel that way for the rest of my life?

"Thank you for the offer," I replied, "but I think it would be better for me to leave, for now."

Why did I add that "for now"? To be polite, or to hold on to hope?

"Let's go," I said to Kadee. I did not want to face Taro or Jaguar. I wasn't sure where I was going, but if I stayed here until they woke, they could probably convince me to stay forever.

Just outside the door, though, something occurred to me. I turned back to ask, "What will happen to the Shantel?"

"That's really not our concern," Kadee whispered, looking at the slowly waking trainers. I could tell she would also rather be gone before they were able to focus on us, but I wanted an answer.

"You demanded blood price from the Azteka," I said to Jeshickah. "What will happen to the Shantel?"

"He was working for Midnight," Kadee asserted before Jeshickah could speak. "By Midnight's law, a nation is not held responsible for the actions of those they have already exiled for betrayal."

"It seems to me," Jeshickah replied, "that our late guard was not exiled, but rather sent to Midnight on an errand. I will deduct his years of service from the account. I think Shantel royal blood will pay the rest."

She stood and shut the door to the cell in our faces, ending any argument.

"That's going to go over well," Kadee said under her breath.

"Let's get Malachi," I replied. The fact remained that the Shantel had—without my knowledge or consent and with no concern about who might be hurt beyond the vampires—turned me into a plague-bearer. A dozen humans had died, at least, and in some ways it was my fault.

More died than that, I realized, thinking back to Calysta. She had killed herself for freedom before I even realized we were in a cage. And the Shantel didn't deserve to enter a marble cage as punishment.

Alejandra had already gone by the time we stepped into the hall. When we opened the door to the lower cells, we found Malachi standing right behind it.

"Much obliged," he said to Kadee. Then, "Vance . . . I'm sorry."

He had said that to me too often, it seemed. I almost said something sharp, as I had most of the other times, but I realized that no one else was likely to express sympathy. Malachi was probably the only one who would ever understand what the trainers, Midnight's evil masters, had once been to me.

"Thank you," I whispered. "Are you all right now?" The last time I had seen him, he had been completely unresponsive.

"Sometimes the only thing louder than the past is the possible future," Malachi answered unintelligibly. "It's . . . overwhelming." He pushed past us as if desperate for fresh air.

Kadee and I exchanged a glance, then hurried in the same direction. When we caught up to Malachi at the front gates, his eyes still held a wide, dazed expression as he stared up at the stone edifice that was Midnight proper.

Kadee asked, "Where to now, Vance?"

I looked around, but there was no guidance to be found here.

There was only one other place I knew, so that seemed as good a place to start as any. "I guess I will go look for the Azteka," I answered. "I don't know where Alejandra went, but I hope I'll find her in the market. I'm not sure I'll stay, but it's somewhere, for now. Alejandra promised I would be well treated."

Kadee nodded. "You'll have to walk. You don't want Jeshickah accusing you of stealing her horse."

"I could fly part of the way."

"I've seen you fly," Malachi said. "You're slower in the air than you are on the ground. We can walk together until we reach the Obsidian camp—if you trust me."

"You're not worried about my knowing where it is?" I asked.

He shrugged.

"You already know enough to have us all given to Midnight," Kadee answered. "The way I see it, we either have to kill you or trust you. You have the same choice to make about us. *Do* you trust us?"

Did I?

"I don't know," I answered. "I don't seem to be a good

judge of who to trust, but I wouldn't kill someone just because she might hurt me."

"That's fair," she answered.

We started on our way, stepping off the road whenever we heard anyone approach. None of us wanted to be seen, stopped, or spoken to by outsiders.

Malachi froze before I even realized we had reached the Obsidian camp. His gaze was locked with his sister's. I remembered what Torquil had said about Misha sending Malachi away.

He drew back and said to me, "I'll walk you to the market."

"You need to face her eventually," Kadee said, dogging our heels.

"I know. But not yet."

If Misha hadn't driven her brother away, I wondered, would I still be in the greenhouse? Malachi wouldn't have come to the greenhouse that day to escape from the storm. Would Calysta still have killed herself if Malachi hadn't reminded her of who she had once been? Maybe. Probably, eventually. Surely I would have frozen to death in the woods if I had never found him.

Or he might have killed me, I thought, *if he hadn't already been so alone, and felt so guilty.*

I didn't want to think about that.

We reached the market. As soon as we saw the Shantel

stall, we understood the purpose of one of the carts that had passed us during our walk.

The wooden structure was piled with bodies in varying stages of decay. Each wore a black collar and the simple clothes of Midnight's slaves. Beneath, their skin was either black or a putrid gray-green, swollen and split to leak the same foul bile I had seen in the blood of the slave Malachi had killed in front of me. Rotten fluids had leaked across the Shantel trade goods.

Words were scrawled in dark ink at the top of the stall.

"It says, 'These are not our dead,'" one of the nearby Shantel merchants provided. "Midnight gave the pochteca permission to dispose of the corpses, and they chose to leave them here."

"What does it mean?" I asked.

"The Azteka wanted to make it clear who was to blame," the merchant said. "Now I need to take the message back to our king, so he can decide whether to pay for this crime with his blood, or to risk Midnight's consequences for defiance."

"What will he do?" I asked.

"He will probably consult the *sakkri*," he answered. "She provides our spiritual guidance. They will decide together what is best."

"They will decide," Kadee said. "The king and the princes and the *sakkri* will decide. Why don't they ask the hunters, or the merchants, or the mothers and fathers and children whether or not they want to fight?"

"That's why we have leaders," the Shantel merchant replied. "Someone needs to make decisions."

These are not our dead, the Azteka had written. No one would claim them. They were simply casualties of a conflict no one wanted responsibility for. I searched the swollen faces, and recognized too many. Elisabeth's was half visible in the middle of the mass.

"Some of the humans recently rebelled against their king," Kadee remarked, almost idly. "They didn't like the decisions he was making for them, so they got rid of him."

We all stared at the pile of bodies. "Do the Azteka have kings?" I wondered aloud.

"Yes," the merchant answered. "Well, priest-kings, I believe. Bloodwitches from the ruling caste, instead of the pochteca."

"But with all their power, they don't fight either?"

"Come away, Vance," Kadee said, grabbing my arm to pull me back from the merchant.

"No, I want to know." I yanked away from her. "If Midnight does nothing good for any of you, then why do you bow to it? Why do you bow to your kings if they do not fight when you want to fight? Why did the only one of you brave enough to fight need to do so in secret?"

"Look where it got him," the merchant replied. "Look where it got all of us."

Do you know where it almost *got you?* I wondered. I couldn't ask that, though, because no one could know that we had nearly assassinated Jeshickah ... unless, I supposed, we managed to try again. Until that opportunity arose, though, it would be better if we kept the information to ourselves, just as the Shantel deathwitch had done.

How many years had he lived in exile on the faith that an opportunity would come? How many jeers and how much disdain had he suffered, only to fail at the end because the Azteka were too afraid to be blamed for the trainers' deaths?

"What about you?" I asked Kadee and Malachi.

"What about us?" Malachi replied.

"You said the Obsidian guild refused to follow any king. So you end up fighting everyone, dealing with Midnight to protect your own people, scrounging for food and basic necessities."

"Yeah?" Kadee challenged.

"It's just that . . . well, I grew up with every luxury Midnight has to offer." I remembered Malachi's tirade about the serpents' dance, though the words struck me very differently now than they once had. "I don't know how to hunt. I don't know how to survive in the forest. I've almost never gone hungry and I've usually had a soft bed to sleep on."

"I'm aware of that," Malachi replied. He turned his back on me and wondered aloud, "Should we do something about this pile of bodies? It *stinks*."

"Burn it," Kadee replied.

Perhaps they both knew I needed a few moments to complete my thoughts and prepare myself to take this next step. They consulted briefly with the Shantel merchant, then sought kindling, flint, and steel. Midnight's dead—*our* dead—would soon be gone to smoke and ash. Just like the life I had once had.

"I have nothing but the clothes I'm wearing," I said as we all watched the pyre begin, "and I know almost nothing of use, but I learn fast. Will you have me?"

"If we haven't made it clear already," Kadee said, "the Obsidian guild is officially fugitive. We can walk through this market freely because it is considered Midnight's land, but a lot of the shapeshifter nations have decrees to arrest or kill us on sight if we cross into their territory . . . which we do, when we need to. Right now you have an invitation to return to the Azteka. A bloodwitch is barely a step below royalty. Your lifestyle would be more like the one to which you are accustomed."

"Yes, it would be," I replied, thinking of Calysta, and Felix and Elisabeth and Joseph, the children in the east wing, and all the slaves who had cooked for me and cleaned up after me most of my life. I thought about Celeste, who had to be protected and taken care of but would never be considered worthy even of a golden cage. Then I thought about Misha, who had gone into a trainer's cell, and how *for folk like us it's better not to give too much thought* to what happened to her there.

I had been taught that kneeling to Jeshickah was polite, and right, because she was better than I was. Maybe this was the potential Jaguar had seen in me: I didn't want to be polite. I didn't want to be led. I didn't want to be comfortable if that meant I needed to accept that my comfort came by the grace of those who were more important than I could ever be, and on the backs of others who were less than dirt beneath my feet.

"I think it would be *just* like that," I said.

Kadee smiled and shook her head.

"You're in for a rude awakening, little bird."

"At least I'll *be* awake," I countered.

I jumped back as a spark from the Shantel merchants' stall, now turned into a pyre, fell on my arm. As I brushed ash from my skin, Kadee said, "It's nice to meet you, Vance Obsidian." She flung an arm across my shoulders and turned me away from the burning bodies.

"You're mad, Vance," Malachi said. "But welcome to the family."

I turned to see him staring at the fire, a pale shadow in front of the flickering flames. I wondered if he, too, was thinking about his prophecy, in which Misha would take the serpiente throne and Midnight would fall to flames just like these.

As I understood it, the empire had stood in some form

280

for four hundred years. What was the likelihood that our generation would see its end?

And when it fell, would I rejoice, or would I cry?

Only time would tell.

All I knew was, whether the walls were rough stone or golden bars, a quetzal couldn't live in a cage.

Turn the page for a sneak peek
at the second volume in the
Maeve'ra trilogy,

BLOODKIN

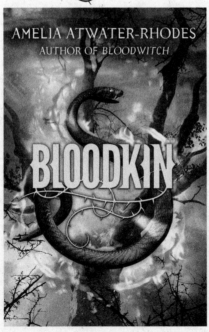

CHAPTER 1

PERFECT WEATHER FOR a shopping trip, I thought as I passed through the gates to the serpiente open-air market.

A fine, chilly drizzle was falling from the overcast May sky. Like everyone else in the market, I kept my head down so the hood of my cloak could keep the rain out of my eyes. Unlike everyone else, I had good reason to hide my face regardless of the weather: like most members of the Obsidian guild, I was wanted for treason. I did have the distinction of being guilty based on my own actions instead of just by association, which was the charge on most of Obsidian's members. I had been convicted at a trial I had declined to attend three years ago—wisely, since the sentence would have been death despite my age.

I was fifteen now, and grateful for the rain.

Under the cloak, I felt half naked in the clothes of a casual serpiente trader: a loose blouse under a half bodice, and trousers that hugged my hips and thighs, then laced even more tightly at my calves. The bodice was low-cut, and dyed a brilliant shade of emerald, leaving the majority of my chest exposed.

A good way to catch your death by lung fever, I thought, then shook my head. The concern was a remnant of another time, another life. Serpent shapeshifters like me were immune to human diseases like that.

Maybe that was why they were so comfortable wearing so little clothing.

Out of the corner of my eye, I spied the black and crimson uniform of a member of the palace guards. His gaze drifted over me as he scanned the crowd in the marketplace, but he paid me no attention. Why would he? I was just another shopper.

Unfortunately, "shopping" was made difficult by the fact that I had no trade goods or currency that I dared use. That meant I had to get creative.

Once, I would have balked at stealing, but these days, my hands were swift. As I moved casually through the marketplace, I took advantage of absentminded shopkeepers—those who were busy flirting, or whose eyes had caught on the brightly dressed dancers who flitted through the crowd. A salt horn, a bag of dried peas, a sack of cornmeal, and a log of goat cheese all disappeared into the haversack that hung at my hip.

I didn't take much from any individual merchant. I couldn't quite resist a warm lamb pie, which smelled of rich spices, but I slipped a blood coin onto the merchant's table where he would find it later.

Midnight called the currency it minted *trade* coins. However, since Midnight was just as quick to trade in slaves as in these pieces of metal, the more evocative name was far more popular. The vampires' empire protected the coins' value, so they were valid even here in the serpiente market, but there was no reason the local trader I was pretending to be would have them. I couldn't afford to draw attention to myself by using them openly, but I didn't like to outright steal something I didn't really *need*.

I was aware that this was a narrow distinction, but I made it anyway.

Food was a necessary resource, but that wasn't the only reason I risked coming to the serpiente market, which was open to the air and sky above but surrounded by high walls on all sides. The only way in or out was through the public areas of the palace, where being caught meant death, but ignorance was even more dangerous. While "shopping," I kept an ear out for gossip. Information was more valuable than gold.

This spring had resulted in a larger than normal number

of healthy lambs born, which was good news. Wool was one of the serpiente's key trade goods. Last year, a winter fever had ravaged the flocks, leaving the serpiente king unable to pay bills owed to masters with neither the patience nor the kindness to offer lenience.

The king had blamed the Obsidian guild. We were already guilty of treason, so why not add a charge of sheep poisoning? It gave him an excuse to send guards into the woods. It gave him an excuse to pay *his* bills with *our* flesh and blood: Shkei and Misha.

I had to stop there in the spitting rain and take a deep breath. Serpiente were very sensitive to the emotions of those around them, and nearby merchants and shoppers had started glancing at me with concern. I couldn't afford the attention. I was here because I was normally *better* than most of our guild at blending in and hiding any anxiety I might feel.

The memory, still raw less than a year later, had taken me by surprise. That was all.

I pretended to examine the trinkets at the nearest merchant's stall as I brought my emotions under control.

A group of dancers, two women and a man, came up beside me. Their bodies were wrapped in brilliantly colored scarves and little else, the cloth just enough to accentuate bare skin that had been painted with henna designs and in some places decorated with tiny rhinestones.

"I'm sorry," the merchant said. "I know I said I would

try to get more of those bone combs for you, but I haven't managed yet."

Bone combs? I wondered. I had seen a few dancers wearing fancy carved combs in their hair but hadn't given much thought to the silly things until now. The Shantel were famous for their bone and leather goods, but the Obsidian guild had a few talented carvers as well, and bone was a material easily acquired through hunting. If this was a popular item that had suddenly become rare, it might be a way to earn a few coins the next time we went to Midnight's market.

I chanced a glance up, and sure enough, one of the women was wearing one of the apparently coveted combs. It had been carved to resemble—what else?—a serpent, with an emerald-green body and a white diamond pattern down its back. The bone had been dyed and polished to such a shine that it glittered like a gem, brilliant against the dancer's dark hair.

As I watched, the snake moved, shifting its coils and blinking its eyes.

Magic, I thought with disappointment. There were people in my guild capable of making and selling a clever carved comb decorated with fancy dyes and varnish, but we couldn't compete with the Shantel magically.

Oh, well.

It was time to move on.

The distraction had helped me compose myself, anyway.

I was walking away when I overheard the words *Obsidian guild*. They hadn't recognized me, or there would have been more shouting, and I knew better than to give myself away by visibly reacting. I discreetly kept my attention on the merchant who had spoken, even as I pretended to stop at another booth.

"I don't know all the details," the merchant said. "All I know is they were involved. They set fire to the Shantel trade stall in Midnight's market. They must have been working with Midnight in some way, or else they would have been picked up by the guards right then for disrupting trade. The Shantel stormed off before I got any more of the story—well, I suppose they had no reason to stay, what with all their goods going up in smoke. Long story short, hopefully they'll have more of those combs next time I go north to market. They might cost a little more," the merchant warned, "since the Shantel lost profitable wares in that fire."

My blood ran cold, in a way that had nothing to do with the rain.

Others had drifted closer, drawn by the gossip, and I let myself join that crowd.

The Obsidian guild was the serpiente boogeyman. While it was certainly true that we lived outside serpiente law—my bag was proof of that—it would have been physically impossible for us to be responsible for every crime the serpiente laid at our door. We were blamed for everything from sick sheep to missing children. Every disaster that befell the serpiente people was put before us, added to a constantly growing tally of unforgivable crimes.

We had been actively hunted ever since the serpiente queen, Elise, had died in a fire. Her three-year-old daughter, Hara, had cried arson, and on the basis of that child's hysterical testimony, every member of the Obsidian guild was suddenly guilty of treason.

This time, though . . .

I had helped set fire to the Shantel market stall. I had done so with their blessing, to make a pyre for the dozen blackened, rotting bodies of human slaves, who had been collateral damage in a Shantel plot to murder the masters of Midnight. The corpses had been piled on the Shantel stall as evidence of their failed treason.

I was one of a very few who knew how close the Shantel had come to succeeding, and what part our guild had actually played in the plot. Malachi, Vance, and I had breathed in the acrid stench of charred blood after magic slew the Shantel witch responsible—the witch *we* had encouraged to take the attack one step further so he could destroy Jeshickah herself. I had feigned ignorance, of course; we all had. Miraculously, Jeshickah had believed us. Her continued belief in that lie was essential to our survival.

I listened long enough to confirm that the current rumor, while unflattering, was no more dangerous than the dozens of crimes of which we had already been convicted.

According to the serpiente, we were bloodtraitors in fact if not by law; we had betrayed our own kind, and were working for the vampires. Rumor said that the Shantel had attempted to fight Midnight, but we had turned them in.

I turned away with my stomach rolling. The merchant, who spoke with the exaggerated drama for which serpiente were famous, made his living trading with Midnight. Yet he called *us* traitors? He probably hadn't complained when the serpiente king sold two of us into slavery less than a year ago.

I returned to the palace gates with my mind heavy but no hesitation visible in my step. I swallowed thickly as I passed the guards, but they saw nothing.

Time to go home.

Hunted, hated ... being in the Obsidian guild wasn't an easy life, but it was a *good* life. I returned to the main camp directly, occasionally pausing to make sure I hadn't been followed, until I passed between two tall fir trees and breathed in the scent of our campfire a little past dusk.

An outsider could have walked through the center of the Obsidian main camp without realizing it was anything but more forest. Even the longhouse, which was large enough for our fifteen members to all sleep there at once—as long as no one wanted privacy or personal space—seemed to blend into the dense evergreen trees and thick, brambly underbrush.

Most of my kin were probably inside now. The sky had

darkened to a dusky purple, and rain was falling heavily enough to make a proper fire impossible outside, so they would have gathered around the longhouse's central hearth to share warmth, as well as the suffocating closeness that serpents always seemed to crave.

I pushed back the oiled skins that served as the longhouse door and was greeted by the heady smell of simmering stew.

"Any problems?" Torquil asked as he extracted himself from the pile of people sprawled in front of the hearth and stood to take the heavy sack of food supplies from me.

Though a simple rat snake, without any of the many strains of power that could be found in our world, Torquil was often jestingly referred to as our "kitchen witch." He possessed the magical ability to turn camp rations into something delicious, even in the latest dredges of winter or now, the earliest bloom of spring, when the nights still tended to drop below freezing and few edible plants were yet available. The stew currently simmering on the hearth smelled like heaven.

"No problems," I answered. "We're being blamed for supposedly betraying the Shantel to Midnight, though."

"Damn." The curse came from Farrell, who had founded the Obsidian guild when he was almost as young as I was now, based on a tribe described in ancient serpiente myths. "I'm sorry, Kadee."

I shrugged. Farrell himself had been accused of

everything from theft to murder to treason and rape—the last being a crime the serpiente viewed as so vile, it did not even merit a trial before execution. He knew what it was like to be vilified for something he hadn't done, without any way to speak up to defend himself.

"We didn't, right?" one of the others asked, sounding half serious. Farrell replied with a glare sharp enough to cut. "Sorry," he said. "If we're going to make the Shantel into another powerful enemy, though, I would like someday to hear the whole story."

"No," Farrell answered flatly, "you wouldn't."

The serpent held Farrell's gaze a moment longer, considering, and then looked at me. "Sorry, Kadee. I know it was bad." He glanced back at Farrell. "I'll trust you. That's all I need to know."

He went back to whittling.

This winter, I had come very close to dying in a cold, dank cell with a bloodstained dirt floor. That cell occupied my all-too-frequent nightmares these days. I had told Farrell the whole story when I returned to the Obsidian camp by the grace of God, and had afterward heeded his advice to keep the details otherwise private, even from the rest of our guild. If the story of our complicity with the Shantel's failed plot ever reached Midnight, we would all be executed, so the fewer people who knew, the safer we all were.

I shoved the sack of supplies at Torquil, then backed out the door. No one chased me, for which I was grateful.

Normal serpiente were never alone. Children stayed with their parents until they were old enough to join communal nurseries. Adults slept in nests with friends, piled on large pillowlike beds without proper form or boundaries, and later took lovers. When distressed, they sought others of their kind and found comfort in the press of skin against skin.

But I was half human, and sometimes I needed to be alone. The other members of the Obsidian guild were the first serpiente I had ever known who respected that decision.

On my way to my own tent, I almost tripped over Malachi, who was sitting in front of the cold, sodden ashes of the central campfire. He seemed to be gazing into a phantom flame only he could see with his pale, blue-green eyes.

Malachi was something like a prophet and holy man and something like an ill relative one takes care of out of a sense of familial responsibility. Despite the damp chill in the spring air, he was wearing nothing but buckskin pants and a dagger at his waist; his shirt, vest, and other weapons lay discarded beside him. His fair skin and white-blond hair looked like silver in the rain, as if he had been carved from precious metals instead of born to a living mother. Glowing indigo symbols writhed across his skin, writing and rewriting themselves on his flesh like slow-moving lightning. Unlike his half siblings, Misha and Shkei, who claimed ignorance of magic, Malachi had undisputed power inherited from his falcon father.

"Hello?" I asked quietly, the way one might call into a darkened room.

Malachi didn't respond. He was focused on the visions dancing behind his eyes. Most of the time, Malachi's trances ended on their own, when he was ready or when he was needed. Over this past winter, though, they had been more common and started to last longer. His brother and sister used to be the most successful at waking him, but Shkei had been gone for almost a year now, and Misha ... *Oh, Misha.* She had been imprisoned in Midnight for months before we had managed to get her back, and her time there had left its mark.

Misha wasn't in the longhouse. She was sleeping in her own tent, with the front flaps closed. That was how she slept every night now.

Twenty-two years ago, Malachi had spoken the prophecy that seemed to define so many of our days: "Someday, my sister, you will be queen," he had said. "When you and your king rule, you will bow to no one. And this place, this Midnight, will burn to ash." By the time I joined them, only three years ago, the guild that refused to bow to any king or priest, and knew no religion higher than day-to-day survival, treated Malachi's prophecy as if it was a holy text. It was why we had done so much, and even sacrificed young Shkei, to get Misha back.

I looked at our prophet, with his gaze lost somewhere in the rain, and at the closed tent where our supposed future queen hid away from the world, and tried to convince myself that I still believed such a future was possible.